MARIE-HÉLÈNE LEBEAULT

THE ACADEMY

THE EVERS SERIES BOOK TWO

BEACHES AND TRAILS
PUBLISHING

To all the Seniors who missed Graduation and Prom because of COVID-19.

ACKNOWLEDGEMENT

Many thanks to the National Novel Writing Month (NaNoWriMo), a yearly challenge that got me writing and has since kept me writing!

CHAPTER I
NEW GIRL

LOLA WAS BEYOND NERVOUS. She was fiddling with the key inside her pocket, debating whether or not to take it out. If she did, a door would appear, and she would have to go through it. Mind you, she wouldn't be going alone. Phyllis, her aunt and legal guardian, would be going with her. In fact, Phyllis was standing right next to her, quietly waiting for her to gather her courage. There hadn't been nearly enough time to prepare for this.

A WEEK AGO, Lola had received a letter of acceptance to a college she hadn't known even existed and a summons to appear at The Academy today for Orientation. Two weeks before that, Lola had left the home she shared with her mother in Baltimore to move into the Evers mansion in Williamsburg, Virginia. Her aunt had graciously taken her in after her mother died. There, she had met her father, dead for over thirteen years, who had traveled to the future with his key. They had yet to figure out how he had done it. On the day of her sixteenth birthday, he had vanished back into the past and, though Lola was grateful to have had that time with him, she still missed him.

She had also met and fallen for a boy called Jackson. He lived and worked on the Estate. Mainly, he was their chauffeur, bookkeeper, and groundskeeper, but would perform any number of tasks that Phyllis, and now Lola, required. It had been gently suggested that Lola and Jackson might marry at some point. At first, Lola had balked at the thought, but she had since warmed up to the idea. Jackson was gorgeous and just about perfect in every way. He had not been pleased with the idea of Lola attending a two-week Summer Program for future Custodians at an Academy no one knew about.

"What do you mean you're going to Hogwarts?" he had exclaimed as she held out the letter to him. After reading the letter himself, he looked at Phyllis, shaking the letter a bit too forcefully and asked, "Do you have any idea what this is about?"

Phyllis held a bewildered expression on her face. "Not at all! I've never heard of such a place. Simon and I certainly never attended, and I'd remember if there had been any talk about it at all when I was growing up," she said, clearly upset. She started folding her cloth napkin and rearranging her place setting. As though talking to herself, she said, "I should call Mr. Radcliff and see what he knows about this. Perhaps Boris would know. It seems quite official."

Lola had dumbly followed the conversation, looking from one to the other, vaguely aware that they were talking about her like she wasn't even there and that she should speak up. But she was still in shock and soon their voices faded into the back of her mind. It occurred to her just then, that she had completely forgotten about Jane. She really should go up and see if she was awake. It was bad enough that she had gone to bed without a word after the party the previous night. But she couldn't seem to get up from the table.

Sure, the key could open a door to just about anywhere in the world. That was a fun perk. It had to be magic; there was no other explanation. And the Archives, the ancient book that had produced the incantations they had needed to find Phyllis when she had accidentally been kidnapped, had to be magic as well. But until this very moment, the truth of it hadn't really had time to sink in. Lola had been so excited to meet her time-traveling dad that all that other stuff had seemed secondary. But now she was required to attend not only a magic school in the fall, but magic summer camp in less than a week.

Without a word, Lola had gotten up and headed out of the room, but Jackson then grabbed her arm.

"Lola, are you even listening to us?" he had asked tersely, his mouth tight with barely restrained annoyance.

She cocked her head at him and responded honestly, "Not really. I tuned out after I heard Phyllis mention Mr. Radcliff." When he started to scowl, she quickly added, "Sorry. It's just that I should go wake Jane and apologize for last night."

"No, I'm sorry. I shouldn't be badgering you. It's not your fault and you are understandably in shock. I would be too," he replied in a gentler tone, though his face was still grim. "And don't worry about Jane. We told her you were missing your parents and needed to be alone last night. She retired soon after you," he explained.

Lola nodded, but then found herself standing by the door unsure what to do next

Phyllis seemed to recover first. She got up, downed the rest of her coffee, wiped her mouth primly with her napkin, and announced, "Don't worry, Lola. We'll get to the bottom of this! I'll go call Mr. Radcliff, and if I don't get answers out of him, I'll call Boris. You take care of your guest and put it out of your mind."

As she left, she kissed Lola on the head and gave her arm a squeeze. "Perhaps opening your gifts might take your mind off the topic. There's one from me in there somewhere." She was almost out in the hall when she called back to Lola, "Happy birthday, Lola!"

At that, Lola started to giggle. Soon, she was laughing so hard tears were streaming down her face as she yelled "Happy birthday, Phyllis!" so her aunt could hear her in the hall leading to the Library. Her sides were hurting, and she was panting. Jackson knelt down beside her and asked if she was having a nervous breakdown.

"No, of course not. Though this might be a delayed reaction to everything that's happened to me in the last couple of months or so," she said, sobering up.

Lola had gone upstairs to fetch Jane and the two of them had then spent the day opening gifts and just hanging out. They'd had a late lunch but all too soon it had been time for Jane to go home and she and Jackson took Jane to the bus stop.

It had taken a couple of days, but they eventually came to the bottom of the summons to the Academy. Mr. Radcliff had no information to share even after a conversation with the elder Mr. Radcliff. Boris, however, had much to share. He was appalled to learn that neither Simon nor Phyllis had attended the Academy though he said he wasn't surprised because they were Americans. Phyllis, clearly offended by her paramour's obvious disdain for her origins, had relayed to Lola and Jackson that all the children of key-bearing families attended the Summer Program from age thirteen to seventeen to learn about the Ancestors and how to use the key responsibly.

Potential Custodians were automatically enrolled in the Academy either after completing high school, or upon the death of the current Custodian. Since Simon had not attended the Academy and had continued to use his key to travel not only through space but through time as well, the Academy was only notified of his death upon Lola's sixteenth birthday.

Lola had been astonished at how quickly the letter had appeared in their home, but then again, it had to be magic. Apparently, she should present herself with her legal guardian at the appointed time and all questions would be answered. She would then be allowed to return home to pack and say goodbye to her family before once more heading to the Academy for her two-week stay.

BACK IN THE PRESENT, Lola took a deep breath, pulled out the key, and thought *The Academy*. A door appeared. Phyllis smiled and took her hand. With the other, she reached out and opened the door.

CHAPTER 2
THE ACADEMY

THE DOOR OPENED into what looked like a large Main Hall. Turning, Lola noticed the door had them enter near the actual entrance, a pair of huge double oak doors, one of which was open to let the afternoon air in. The air was cooler than at home in the south; the first clue to the Academy's location.

Taking in her surroundings, she saw the Hall opened onto three rooms: two on either side and a third straight ahead, all featuring over-sized French doors. She couldn't see inside the rooms as the windows were frosted. Lola was imagining grand ballrooms and sitting rooms like the ones in her favorite Jane Austen novels. On either side of the middle room were two massive staircases leading to the second floor. That's when she saw some tables had been set up and where people were lining up in front of them.

Without speaking, Lola and Phyllis settled in line. Teens were appearing through doorways with their parents and rushing to join one another in joyful greeting. Lola observed the arrivals, spinning her head in all directions to try to take it all in and hoped to see someone looking as out of place as she felt. She was so absorbed with the flutter of activity around her, that she didn't notice they were now at the front of the line until someone barked, "Name?"

Lola jumped and immediately started to apologize. "I'm sorry, it's my first . . ." as she turned back to look at the person making this request. She never got a chance to finish her sentence because there, seated at the table, asking for her name rather rudely was a very small man with an exceptionally huge beard. Lola reached for Phyllis but was soon out for the count on the floor.

She awoke in a small room with some sort of nurse pressing a cool cloth to her forehead.

"Phyllis?" she asked in a panic.

"Here I am, darling," replied Phyllis as she drew closer. "You fainted! You get that from me, to be sure."

The nurse was flashing a light in both of her eyes and then asked her to follow her finger with her eyes. Satisfied with Lola's performance, she declared there was no concussion and asked Lola if she felt well enough to sit up. As Lola sat up, she noticed there was another person in the room with them. A tall, ethereal-looking man with long white hair, though he did not look old enough to have hair so white, smiled at her. When she smiled back, he tucked a strand of his hair behind his very pointy ear and winked at her. Lola was obviously not up on her fantasy folklore. *If this is an Elf, what the heck was that other thing sitting at the table?*

The lovely man approached, bent down, and took her hand. "Welcome to the Academy, Lola. I'm Headmaster Lianon," he said kindly.

"Hello, sir," was all Lola could stammer out. Boris had not mentioned anything about Elves!

"I know this can be a lot to take in, even for younger students who have been prepared. If you feel well enough, I'd like to show you around personally. Your aunt has your information packet and you've been checked in," he said as he held out his hand.

Lola looked at Phyllis, who waving a leather-bound folder and nodding encouragingly. She took the proffered hand and stood up. Though she felt fine and steady, he did not relinquish her hand but instead placed it on his forearm and offered his other to Phyllis.

"Ladies, shall we?" he said, and they left the little room. Lola realized they were back in the Hall. She hadn't noticed the doors leading to rooms under the stairs and made a mental note to investigate later.

The tour lasted about an hour and Headmaster Lianon took them to a few of the classrooms. Most were rather small and would accommodate no more than fifteen students at a time. He ran through the curriculum Lola would be expected to complete in the fall and she was disappointed to learn it contained the usual subjects she would have taken in her senior year at any other school. At her crestfallen look, the Headmaster assured her there would be more advanced classes after the first semester when she began her college-level classes.

"You mean I'm going to complete my senior year in one semester?" she asked incredulously.

"I've seen your school transcripts. You are an excellent student so I don't see how that will be a problem. Do you?" he asked, raising an eyebrow.

"No, of course not, sir. I'll do my very best," she replied quickly.

"Wonderful!" he said and off they went to visit the Dining Room and the Common Room. Those were the rooms that led off the Main Hall. He also showed them the Library before bringing them back to where they started.

"I'll leave you in the capable hands of one of our student-volunteers. Sara here will tell you about the Summer Program and show you the second floor where you will find your room for the next two weeks," said the Headmaster as he took Phyllis's hand in his and gave it a quick shake.

"Ms. Evers, do let me know if there is anything I can do to assist you further," he told Phyllis. She thanked him, as did Lola, and he went off to greet other families. Meanwhile, Sara was beaming and clutching her clipboard.

"You must be Lola Evers. Hello, I'm Sara Dunham. I'm from Gloucester. Lovely to meet you!" she said with the telltale posh British accent while holding out her hand.

Lola shook it awkwardly and smiled back. "Hi, I'm from Baltimore, but I live in Williamsburg, now. This is my aunt Phyllis," she added, motioning to Phyllis.

"How do you do, Ms. Evers. Please, follow me," she said as she led them up one of the staircases. When they reached the top, she explained that the boys' rooms were on the left and girls' were on the right. As they walked down the hall, Sara pointed out the girls' restrooms and shower rooms. There was also a common Sitting Room with a fireplace and a small kitchen for light snacks and beverages. All proper meals were served in the Dining Room at set times and Lola was reminded that students should never be late.

Eventually, Sara stopped at number fourteen.

"Home, sweet home," she said as she pulled out a key from her pocket and opened the door. Then she handed the key to Lola and held the door for Lola and Phyllis.

It looked like a typical college Dorm Room. There was a large window in the center of the room with two desks arranged on either side. Twin beds were pushed against opposite walls and bookcases sat back to back in the middle of the room to provide a little privacy. The bed on the left had a frilly pink bedspread and there was a large cedar chest at the end of the bed.

"Your roommate has already arrived and claimed the left side of the room," she said. "Can you guess who it is?" she added rocking back and forth on her heels and barely suppressing a squeal.

"You?" guessed Lola.

"Correct!" she cooed. "Isn't it fantastic?" she added.

At a loss for words, Lola smiled and looked at Phyllis, who had walked over to the window to peer out at the grounds. Seeing Lola's tight smile, Phyllis replied for her.

"That's wonderful news, Sara! This way Lola will have a friend to usher her through the first couple of days until she meets the other students," Phyllis said with enthusiasm.

Sara beamed again, pleased. "I should warn you; we won't be in the same classes even though we are the same age. I've been coming here every summer since I was thirteen and you'll need to catch up. But we can go down to meals together and I'll introduce you to all my friends and show you the lay of the land—never fear!" she said reassuringly.

"Right," she continued briskly, "here is your schedule. I've given you the key, what's missing?" Tapping her upper lip and frowning in concentration, her face then lit up. "Ah yes, the school uniform. In your information packet, there is a sizing sheet. Fill it out when you get home, then fold it into a triangle. It will be sent back immediately, and your items will be here waiting for you when you get back," she explained. Sara retrieved a piece of paper from her desk drawer and demonstrated how to fold it. Lola and Phyllis observed this with great interest. It looked like origami.

"The dress code is on the back of the schedule along with the rules. But the most important rule you need to know right now is that you may not leave the school grounds by any means while enrolled in the Summer Program unless authorized by a teacher or the Headmaster. However, you may have visitors between one and four p.m. on Sundays," she concluded with a wink.

Lola took this in. No Phyllis for a week. No Jackson for a week. Then she asked nervously, "Can I call or text if I need something?"

Sara looked pained. "There is no mobile service here. There's an ancient telephone system, but it only works within the school," she said. "You'll need to write a letter, which will be verified by the censor committee before being sent. But once sent, it will arrive instantly to the sender. It's super quick!" she exclaimed, snapping her fingers.

Lola pondered this and looked at Phyllis who wore an identical worried expression to her own.

"It's all in your information packet," Sara added encouragingly. Then she looked at the time and added, "If you want to have time to pack and read through those papers, you should get a move on. You need to be back here by dinner, which is served promptly at six p.m. That means you'll need to deposit your things here and change before you go down. I'll wait for you." She smiled as she walked to the door and opened it.

Lola looked at her own watch and saw it was already three p.m. "Thanks, I appreciate it. I'll be here no later than five-thirty," she promised. They left the room and went back down to the Main Hall.

"Always travel to and from the Hall with your key," advised Sara. "See you later, Lola. It was nice meeting you, Ms. Evers," she added as she waited for them to leave.

Lola took the traveling key out, thought of home and they were off.

CHAPTER 3
GETTING READY

WHEN LOLA and Phyllis got home, they wordlessly went to Lola's room to begin packing. Once inside, and with the door closed, they both sank onto her sitting room sofa. It took a few minutes before either of them was able to form a coherent thought. Eventually, Phyllis opened the information packet and started reading the rules out loud.

Academy Rules

1. Only registered students and authorized staff are permitted on campus.

2. Parents and visitors, unless summoned, are welcome on Sundays from one to four p.m. and must arrive and depart from the Main Hall. They must also sign in and out of the Register.

3. Electronic devices will not function and are prohibited.

4. Alcohol, drugs, and tobacco are strictly prohibited on campus.

5. Students shall be in uniform at all times while on campus. Casual attire is permitted within their respective dormitories.

6. Students must attend all classes, meals, and assemblies that they are scheduled for.

7. Students shall maintain decorum and good behavior at all times.

8. Students must remain in their dormitories between ten p.m. and six a.m.

9. Boys and girls must remain in their respective dormitories.

10. Students shall make every effort to achieve academic and personal success.

"That sounds fair," replied Lola, and Phyllis went on to read the Dress Code aloud.

Academy Dress Code

1. All students are required to wear the prescribed school uniform and modifications to the uniform are not permitted.

2. All students wearing the school uniform are to ensure that their shirt is tucked in at all times. Students are expected to keep their appearance neat and tidy.

3. Students may not accessorize their uniforms and should be discreet with personal adornment, whether jewelry, hairstyle, or makeup. Hats are not permitted.

Phyllis was nodding as she then read out the items for Lola's school wardrobe. "That seems reasonable. Have you ever worn a school uniform?" she asked.

"No, but I've seen plenty of movies where they do, and the description doesn't sound too bad. Though I don't know why there aren't any skirts," replied Lola.

"Probably to avoid showing too much leg or having to offer the skirt in male sizes to be politically correct," suggested Phyllis.

Lola burst out laughing as she imagined some boys wearing the skirt with fashionable stockings and flair, while others wore it like a kilt with their hairy legs sticking out from under it. She shared the joke with her aunt and they both chuckled. As Lola turned the paper over to the schedule, her face became serious again.

"Alright, I've got a class tomorrow morning called *History of Magical Artifacts* followed by *Latin for Incantations* and *Magical Communities*," said Lola deadpan. "I guess I did not hallucinate the Dwarf registrar and the Elf Headmaster?" she added.

"I'm afraid not, because I saw them too. I wonder if the whole faculty is, well, um, different," replied Phyllis.

"I guess there is only one way to find out!" Lola said as she got up.

"I should start packing. Do you have a suitcase I can borrow?" she asked, heading towards her room.

Phyllis followed suit and replied, "You can use the chest at the end of your bed. You'll find packing boxes under the extra blankets and pillows."

Lola walked to the chest, peered inside, and smiled. She removed the blankets and pillows and took out the packing boxes and soft cubes. She put the blankets on one of the armchairs and arranged the boxes and cubes on her bed.

"I don't need to bring that much stuff because of the uniform. Oh, that reminds me, I need to fill in the sizing sheet, do you have it?" she asked.

Phyllis went back to the sitting room to retrieve the information packet. She found the sizing sheet and a convenient packing list. "There's a packing list! Here, look it over while I go get a measuring tape from my room," said Phyllis.

Lola read the list and called out to her aunt, "Do I have a toiletry bag?"

Phyllis was already at the door, but she called out, "Under the sink in your bathroom. Back in a minute."

Lola went to the bathroom with the list and put everything she needed in the toiletry bag. She then packed some towels into one of the boxes. Grabbing a packing cube, she neatly folded her underwear, pajamas, and robe. There were some shoe bags, so she used those for her slippers and her favorite Chucks. She tossed in her jeans, a couple of t-shirts and some socks, just in case. She went up to her alcove and got some pens and pencils, as well as a few of the leather-bound journals, for notes.

She was about to come down when she thought of Jane. *How am I going to explain this to Jane?* After opening the laptop and browser, she started composing an email to her best friend.

From, lola4evers@gmail.com
To, jane173@gmail.com
Hey Jane!
I'm going to have to keep this short as I'm pressed for time. I'm leaving

for a two-week stay at some kind of summer camp, which doesn't allow any devices. So, I won't be in touch for a bit, but I will tell you everything when I get back! Promise!

Luv u

Lola

xoxoxo

She heard Phyllis coming back downstairs and went down to join her. She was wondering what to put her supplies in, since her backpack didn't seem nice enough, and they wouldn't fit in any of the snazzy purses Phyllis had given her.

"Sorry I took so long. I stopped by your father's room to get you his satchel," she said, holding out a leather messenger bag.

"That's perfect!" Lola cried as she opened the flap and placed her supplies inside it. On impulse, she brought the bag to her face and inhaled deeply, hoping it would smell like Simon, but it only smelled like well-worn leather.

"Do you think I could bring one of the yoga mats?" she asked Phyllis.

"Yes, of course, darling. And perhaps a book or two, just in case the school library only has academic volumes," she suggested.

"Good thinking!" Lola replied.

"Let's get these measurements out of the way. I'm very excited about seeing the paper disappear!" said Phyllis.

They measured Lola and filled out the sizing sheet. Then, Lola took the folded paper from her pocket that Sara had given her and replicated the folds with the sizing sheet. They stood there staring at the triangle, just waiting.

"Nothing's happening," whispered Lola.

"Perhaps it needs to be addressed?" suggested Phyllis in a louder whisper.

Lola unfolded the paper and looked for extra instructions. Nodding her head, she refolded it, got a pen, and wrote *The Academy–Uniforms* on it and took a step back, expectantly.

A gust of wind lifted the triangle swiftly and just before it hit Lola in the face, it disappeared.

"Unbelievable!" breathed Lola.

"Indeed!" replied Phyllis then said, "Alright, we made good time. It's almost four p.m. Is everything packed? When is Jackson coming over?"

"Yes, and I told him to come at four-thirty. I figured we'd be home by then," Lola said as she checked the list one last time to ensure she had everything. She went to her bedside to put her phone on the charge; she wouldn't be needing it for a while. She did the same with her iPad. When she turned back, Phyllis was looking at her expectantly. "Sorry, did you say something?" she asked.

"What are you going to tell Jackson?" asked Phyllis. "About the *Magical Communities...*" she trailed.

Lola bit her lip and said, "I'm not sure. I didn't know what to tell Jane, so I said I was going to summer camp for two weeks, that devices weren't allowed, and I'd fill her in when I got back. Which is true, to a point. But Jackson already knows this is some kind of magic school. What do you think I should say?"

Phyllis thought about it for a moment, then replied, "We don't know how much of this we're meant to keep secret. Maybe we've already crossed a line with Jackson. So I think you should keep it simple. Once you know more about it, you'll be better prepared to handle any questions that might come up. Including whether or not Jackson can visit you next Sunday."

"Oh, I didn't think of that. Family and visitors will arrive by the door, which implies they either have a key or are allowed to accompany someone who has a key. But wait, maybe people will arrive by car and use the front door. Where exactly is the school?" asked Lola.

"I asked the Headmaster while they took you to the infirmary. He was quite vague. He actually said, '*It's neither here, nor there.*' So that must mean it's out of time and space. Or in another dimension? My head hurts when I try to think of this. I wish Simon were here. He's so much better at this sort of thing than I am," said Phyllis, rubbing her temples.

Lola went over to give her aunt a hug. "Me too. Come and help me choose some books to pack while I wait for Jackson," she suggested, and they went down together.

CHAPTER 4
SAYING GOODBYE

"WHAT TIME DO you have to go?" asked Jackson, as he wrapped his arms around Lola and his lips brushed a kiss on her forehead. Her hand slipped into his as she led him to the sofa in her sitting room. They sat, hips touching, hands interlaced.

"I guess I should leave by five-fifteen. I told my roommate I'd be there by five-thirty to drop off my stuff and change into our school uniform before dinner," said Lola, her thumb absently rubbing the skin between his thumb and forefinger.

His head jerked up and he turned to face her. "Wait, what? Back up a minute. Roommate? School uniform? Start at the beginning," said Jackson, his eyes wide in alarm.

Lola bit her bottom lip, biding her time while thinking about what to say.

She filled her lungs up and dove in. "Right. Remember when I said I was going to Hogwarts? Well, there are more similarities than I initially imagined. First, it's like a private school. They have rules, a uniform, and separate boys' and girls' dormitories. Each room has two people, hence the roommate. My roommate's name is Sara and she seems nice," Lola concluded with an exhale.

Jaw twitching, Jackson nodded and said, "Go on." There was a crease between his brows, but he didn't look angry. Lola continued, "There is also a ban on technology, though I think it's more a case of technology just doesn't work there. I'm still not sure where *there* is. The Summer Program lasts two weeks, and I'll have to stay on campus for the whole time. Visitors are allowed on Sundays from one to four p.m., but I don't know yet if that extends to non-keyholders. I'll keep you posted." Lola wrung her hands and waited for his reaction.

Jackson's brows furrowed closer together, but he said nothing at first. He seemed to be digesting the information. Lola waited as butterflies flew willy nilly in her stomach. She checked her watch while Jackson's gaze was fixed on the coffee table. When he turned to look at her, his brows were smooth, and he was smiling. Lola sighed with relief. She didn't know exactly what was making her so uneasy, but she didn't want to leave for two weeks and have things be awkward with Jackson.

He took both her hands and said, "If you're okay with it, I'm okay with it. I can't wait to hear all about it."

Lola was so relieved he wasn't pushing for more information and asking a bunch of questions that she pounced on him and threw her hands around his neck. The force of her enthusiasm knocked Jackson back onto the sofa seat cushions. Heads bumping, they burst out laughing. Jackson's arms snaked around her waist and pulled her closer. Since her arms were still around his neck, it brought her face inches from his. Their eyes locked. She grew breathless, anticipating the kiss that hung in the air between them. It had been hanging there for weeks now. Lola was afraid he would break away and act all gentlemanly and she just couldn't take it anymore. Quickly, before she lost her nerve, or he moved his head, she kissed him. His lips were warm but unyielding at first. She pressed her full weight onto him, her hands grasping the back of his head. He groaned. His lips parted slightly, and he returned the kiss. A triumphant moan escaped Lola's lips.

His hands moved up and down her back. Then he settled a hand on her lower back as the other tangled in her hair. He drew her closer still. Lips parted further and tongues met. Lola made a soft mewling sound. *We are French Kissing!* She never wanted it to stop. He tasted so good; she could swallow him whole. Her skin was on fire as her body melted onto him like ice cream on pie. There was a faint nudge coming from his pants and she stilled. Then she gave a nervous giggle that completely killed the mood. Jackson slowly ended the kiss by lightly sucking her bottom lip as he moved his arms down her back then up her arms where he seized her hands to untangle them from around his neck. He kept hold of her hands and smiled at her as he sat up. Back to reality.

"I think that's as steamy as I can take right now," said Jackson slightly out of breath.

Lola looked at him and bit her lip. "That was amazing! Could you tell it was my first real French Kiss?" she stammered. She felt like she was on the verge of babbling uncontrollably.

Jackson kissed each of her hands and put them on her lap. "That *was* amazing, and you are a natural," he assured her. Then he got up and moved away from the sofa and checked his watch. "I would have preferred our first *real* kiss not happen moments before you leave for two weeks during which we won't be able to communicate," he added as he raked his hands through his hair.

Lola got up too. Her legs felt rubbery and she wavered a bit. Jackson was near her in an instant, holding an arm out to steady her. She smiled up at him, her gaze was dewy and lovestruck. Jackson shook his head, brought her in for a hug, and gave her a kiss on the temple. "What am I going to do with you?" he asked with a sigh.

There was a knock at the door and moments later Phyllis came in. Neither of them moved other than to turn their heads towards the door.

"Am I interrupting?" asked Phyllis, innocently. She didn't wait for an answer and continued, "Lola, I believe it's time to go. And, as it's close to five p.m., I'm afraid we'll have to say our goodbyes here and now."

Lola let go of Jackson and moved into Phyllis's open arms. "I'm going to miss you, Phyllis," she said.

"Me too, darling. I've grown quite attached to you and your presence here. But we'll be fine; it's only for two weeks. And I'll see you next Sunday. Go. Have fun, make friends and you can tell us all about it when we see you next," said Phyllis and she released Lola, wiping a small tear from her eye.

Lola turned to Jackson and gave him a teary smile. "I'll miss you too, Jackson," she said.

Jackson took her face in his hands and gave her a quick kiss on the forehead. Then, he put his hands on her shoulders and said, "Stay aware, be observant, and try to stay out of trouble."

Lola burst out laughing. Soon they were all laughing, and the tension drained out of the moment. "It'll be fine. I'll be with a bunch of kids much younger than me. If their parents let them go to magic camp for two weeks every summer, I'm pretty sure it'll be safe for me to go," she said more confidently than she felt.

She had sent her trunk through the door earlier, as per the instructions in her information pack. It would apparently be waiting for her, with her uniform, when she got to her room. There was really nothing left to do but take out her key and go through the door.

CHAPTER 5
DINING ROOM

WHEN LOLA OPENED the door to her Dorm Room, the first thing she noticed was her chest at the foot of her bed and her uniform folded neatly on it, with both pairs of shoes looking shiny and new.

"You're here!" said Sara as she dropped the book she'd been reading and flew off her bed to greet Lola. She seemed to be about to hug Lola but thought better of it.

"Welcome to your new home!" she said clapping her hands together and jumping up and down in excitement. "Hurry up and change. I'd like to go down a little earlier to introduce you to a few people," she said.

When Lola just stood there, she added, "Don't be shy, I can't see you from my bed because of the bookcase. But you can go change in the restroom if you prefer." Sara plopped on her bed and resumed reading, or pretending to read, her book.

Lola snapped out of it and quickly changed into the clean, starched items from her chest. She opted for the polo and cardigan combo. She wasn't sure about the tie, and the blazer seemed too stuffy. The clothes were comfortable and fitted well. She walked over to the mirror hanging on the wall next to the door.

"How do I look?" she asked Sara tentatively.

"Lovely, you'll fit right in. Now, come on! Don't forget your room key," said Sara, already opening the door.

Lola had put her traveling key on a navy ribbon around her neck and had brought a red one for the room key. That way she was sure she would never lose either and the ribbons accessorized with the uniform. She lifted them up and out of her polo shirt to show Sara, who responded by lifting her own keys on gold and silver chains around her neck. She motioned for Lola to pass and closed the door behind her.

The corridor was loud with the chatter of girls catching up as they all headed down to dinner. When they reached the staircase, boys started filing out of their dormitory and heading down the opposing staircase.

The combination of navy, vermillion, and crisp white was lovely to see. Lola wondered why more schools didn't have uniforms. Everyone looked neat and tidy and it cut down on the time it took to select an outfit.

Sara was telling Lola about her home in Gloucester, England. She lived in an old cottage with her parents and two younger sisters, Eva, aged ten, and Glenda, aged eight. Lola was about to ask about the age difference when Sara said, "Mum remarried when I was four and Leonard, my step-dad, is the only father I've ever known. My father died when I was a baby. I don't remember much about him."

"I'm sorry to hear that. You get along with Leonard, then?" asked Lola.

"Yeah, we're thick as thieves. It's like he gets me better than Mum sometimes," she replied ruefully.

Once they got to the bottom of the stairs, they followed the others into the Dining Room. From the size of the room and the ornate ceiling and wall sconces, Lola presumed it used to be a ballroom. The four long banquet tables were set to receive a dozen or so students. They seemed to be grouped by age. Sara grabbed her hand and pulled her to one of the tables and they sat down. The conversation around the table died down and everyone turned to Lola expectantly.

"Everyone, this is Lola Evers, our newest recruit. She's from the U.S.A.," said Sara.

Lola smiled shyly and gave a small lame wave as Sara continued with the introductions.

"This is Lenora. She's from Ireland." Sara pointed to a tall, pale girl with straight, limp red hair parted down the middle. When Lenora opened her mouth to greet her, Lola immediately noticed her braces. Her very green braces.

Next was a handsome boy with blue eyes and longish, black hair tied back loosely. His straight, white teeth gleamed when he smiled at Lola. "This here is Colin, he's also Irish," said Sara. Colin reached out his hand to take Lola's and kissed it. "*Enchanté*," he said with a wink. Lola blushed and snatched her hand back as she murmured a strangled, "Hi."

Sara laughed and added, "Don't worry, Lola. The lovely young man next to Colin is James who is also Irish—and they've been dating for over a year." James had short brown hair and a pleasant face. He looked wholesome, like the boy next door type. He smiled at Lola and welcomed her to the school.

Seated next to Sara was Clara, a French girl, who was so beautiful Lola wondered if she was a model. She had long, wavy blond hair cascading down her back, the most piercing green eyes, and an absolutely blinding smile. Before Lola knew what was happening, the girl shot up, flew over, and enveloped her into a tight hug. "*Bienvenue, ma nouvelle amie!*" she exclaimed, then she kissed her on both cheeks and announced, "We shall be great friends, I just know it." She beamed at Lola, oblivious to the acute discomfort she had caused, and returned to her seat with a graceful hair toss. Seeing Lola's shell-shocked reaction, Sara laughed and elbowed Lola as she whispered, "You'll get used to it. People are very friendly here."

Lola nodded and gathered up enough courage to address the group, "Thank you all so much. I'm happy to be here. This is all very new to me and I hope you'll excuse my total ignorance."

There were other people at the table, but it seemed they were not part of Sara's posse and were not introduced to Lola. The students nodded at her, friendly enough. There was an empty chair next to Lola and she wondered if it would be a new student, like her. She wouldn't feel so conspicuous.

Just then, the lights blinked, and everyone stopped talking and rose. Lola followed suit and craned her neck to see what was going on, as everyone had turned toward the front of the room. There stood another long table, perpendicular to those of the students, much like the bride and groom's table at a wedding, with place settings only on one side. *That must be the Faculty table.*

They filed in one by one and stood behind their chairs. Lola could only stare open-mouthed at the lot of them. From what she could tell, only two of them were, well, human. Both men. The first two ladies were what she could only describe as fairies. Another lady looked like she may be related to the Headmaster. Though she seemed older, she had the same pointy ears and long silvery hair as the Headmaster. Lola recognized the one from the registration table. Beside him was some kind of Dwarf in a kimono and a man-bun. The last to arrive was a huge male with extremely dark, purple skin. He was followed by the Headmaster who headed for the small podium and addressed the assembly.

"Welcome to the 2019 Summer Program. I see our newest group of recruits are all present and accounted for," he said, pausing to wave gingerly at the table full of giggling 13-year-olds. "You will also note that we have a few older students that are new, as is want to happen when the legacy is a surprise to family members," he continued and waved to no one in particular. Lola was very grateful for that. She'd had as much attention as she could stand for at least two or three lifetimes.

"Let me introduce you to our Summer Faculty. Please welcome Professor Elderberry. She is our new Herbology teacher. Next to her is Professor Brambles, our returning Mindfulness and Meditation teacher. Also joining us once more on our Faculty is Lady Samsara from the Department of Traveling and Doctor McClary of the History Department. More familiar faces are Doctor Thompson, our Latin teacher, Sir Kravchuk, our Magical Communities teacher, and Master Smoke, our resident Martial Arts professor. Finally, we would like to introduce Professor Thunderbolt, our new Magic teacher. Let's give them all a welcoming hand," he said, clapping.

All the students clapped, and the teachers were seated. The Headmaster nodded to someone on the sidelines and a fleet of servers filed out and deposited large, covered silver platters on each table. The Headmaster went to his own seat, and as he shouted, "*Bon Appétit*," the servers removed the silver covers and departed. The students sat and started to eat, resuming their conversations.

It was quite a feast! One platter had roasted potatoes, parsnips, carrots, and cabbage. Another held dinner rolls, butter rosettes, and a selection of hard cheeses. Further down the table was sliced turkey breast in gravy, breaded veal cutlets, and Polish sausages. For dessert, there were cupcakes and an assortment of fresh fruit cups. Whoever had the platter in front of them would serve everyone else and plates were passed around as people shouted what they wanted. It was total chaos. It was like those large family gatherings Lola saw in movies. Except everyone at their table was 16–18 years old. Unnerved, Lola was holding her plate, staring at the spectacle, wondering how to proceed. It was like waiting to jump on a merry-go-round.

She felt someone slide in next to her, take her plate, and say, "Allow me." Lola turned her head to look at the newcomer who had already passed her plate to Colin.

"What would you like?" he asked. When she only stared at him, open-mouthed, he said, "A bit of everything?" Lola nodded dumbly. He made the requests and introduced himself as he did. This was the most unusual boy she had ever seen. Firstly, he was extremely tall. Even seated, he had to bend down to speak to her. He was also lithe and wiry. His skin was so pale she could see the veins right through it. He had curly blond hair that was so pale it was almost white. It framed his face like a halo. Just when she thought he might be an albino, he turned to her and smiled as he set the plate in front of her. His eyes were the palest blue, but his eyelashes and eyebrows weren't white like an albino's, they were a golden blond, a shade darker than his hair.

Lola thanked him and blurted out, "I'm Lola, from the U.S." To which he replied with an accent she couldn't place, "I'm Devlin. A pleasure to meet you, Lola. I am from Sweden." He got his own plate back and they started eating. The food was delicious and Lola was ravenous. Which was surprising considering how nervous she was. Soon, she was asking for seconds of everything and Devlin laughed and exclaimed, "I love a woman with an appetite!"

Lola was feeling a little self-conscious. Sara leaned into her and whispered, "Do you think he fell down from heaven?"

CHAPTER 6
COMMON ROOM

AT EIGHT P.M., the lights blinked to signify the end of the evening meal. Anyone still hungry had to hurry and fill their plates as the servers came back out to remove the trays. Most of the students and Faculty members got up and left. Sara told Lola that they could stay in the Dining Room until eight-thirty. No tea or coffee was served there, Sara had told her, as it was served in the Common Room for the students and in the Faculty Lounge for the adults. *They probably also had port and brandy!*

"Are all meals served on fine china with crystal glassware?" asked Lola as the majority of the people at their table got up to leave.

"Breakfast, served from six-thirty to eight-thirty a.m., is buffet-style. Lunch, served from twelve forty-five to two-fifteen, is a seated affair, though with lighter fare," was Sara's reply.

"Oh, thanks. I'm glad it's not a big thing in the morning. I'm not used to interacting with humans that early. On another note, is it me, or do all the girls have names that end in an *a*?" asked Lola.

Sara beamed and exclaimed, "That's right. You don't know anything about that!"

Lola looked at her askance and said, "So it's a thing?"

"Yes, it's quite THE thing," replied Sara. "Are you done eating? I can tell you about it on the way. Do you want to go to the Common Room or back to the Dorm?" she asked.

Lola had had enough socializing for one day. She knew she would see plenty of people in her classes tomorrow. "Up to the room, if you don't mind," she replied.

WHEN THEY GOT to the room, Lola took out her class schedule and asked Sara about it. "How do the classes work? I mean, there are four classes in the morning and two in the afternoon. I can see that," she stated.

Sara went to plop down on her bed on her stomach. Then she lifted the side of her bedspread and took out a box from under her bed. From it, she took out a plastic food container. She pushed the box back under the bed, opened the container, and held it out to Lola. "Contraband?"

Lola walked over to peer into the container. It was full of colorful candy. She grabbed a wine gum and a jelly baby. "Thanks. Why didn't I think to bring candy!" Sara motioned for her to sit on her bed. Taking a bite out of her licorice, she pointed to Lola's schedule.

"There are four one-hour theoretical classes in the morning with five-minute breaks between them. The theoretical classrooms are all in the eastern wing so it's easy to get from one to another." Sara then pointed to the room numbers. "See here, E-121, E is for east. To situate you, the girls' dormitory is the second floor of the west wing, while the boys are in the east.

"In the afternoon, there are two classes of one hour and fifteen minutes with a fifteen-minute break in between. One is a practical class and one is a physical education class. The break is longer as there can be some distance between the two," said Sara. Then she pointed to Lola's schedule again and added, "Practical classes are in the west wing, see here W-144. Physical education classes are usually outside. Either way, students meet the teachers in the Main Hall."

Lola was nodding, looking at her schedule, then looking out the window. "What about when it rains? It just occurred to me that there wasn't any outerwear included in the uniform and we weren't asked to bring any," said Lola, perplexed.

Hands clapping and bouncing on the bed in excitement, Sara said, "That's right! I keep forgetting it's your first time here. What fun!" Then she sat cross-legged and took a deep breath and announced, "The Headmaster controls the weather."

Lola looked at her dumbly. When she didn't react or respond, Sara continued, "It never rains and it's always sunny. It's basically always 22-degrees Celsius. All day, every day."

Lola's brows knit together. "But how do things grow without rain?" she asked.

At this, Sara howled with laughter and fell back on her bed, laughing so hard she clutched her stomach. Eventually, the mirth died down and she got back up with a straight face. "I do apologize. I really wasn't making fun of you," she said contritely.

Lola shrugged and replied, "That's okay. But what was so funny?"

Sara shook her head in disbelief. "Things grow with magic, of course. Most things at The Academy are done with magic." Sara reached for the small plant she had on her desk and held it on her palm. With the other hand, the tips of her fingers brushed her lips and she blew a kiss to the plant. As Lola stared, transfixed, a small white flower bloomed. Her hands flew to her mouth in astonishment. Seconds later, the bloom disintegrated and rose in a cloud of mist.

Lola's face fell and her lips puckered. "Where did it go?" she asked, clearly disappointed.

Sara laughed and put the plant back on her desk. "It's an illusion," she said. "Like everything else here." Lola's eyes were still fixed on the plant, bemused.

Her head shot up as one of her pressing questions came to her. "Right. While we're on the topic. Where, exactly, is *here*?" asked Lola.

"Oh, my," was Sara's reply. "There is no *here*, per se. This is a magical world. A safe world created specifically for The Academy. It's essentially the size of the grounds."

"If I were to walk to the end of the grounds, what would happen?" Lola asked, fascination etched on her face.

"You would bounce off an invisible barrier. Like a dome," responded Sara. "You'll see it when you go outside for your physical education class tomorrow," she added.

Lola kicked off her shoes and scooted backwards so that her back rested on the wall. "Wow," she said. "I'm going to need some more candy to process that," she added as she looked at Sara. Her roommate held out the container and Lola grabbed a toffee, a black licorice baby, and a couple of Maltese balls. "I'll ask my aunt to bring some candy to share when she visits," she said as she popped one of the candies in her mouth. Sara waved her away.

"I can't imagine how you must be feeling. My whole family attended The Academy, for generations. It's really become ho-hum to us. What I wonder is why your family didn't attend?" asked Sara.

Lola shook her head. "I have no idea. And I'm pretty sure both my dad and my aunt didn't even know it existed. From what I can tell, they've been passing keys down to children when they turned thirteen, gave them a few guidelines and that was it."

Sara thrust the container back at Lola who smiled in appreciation and grabbed a few more candies. She waited for Lola to resume.

"I mean, my dad managed to travel back in time to be with me just before I turned sixteen, so that was cool. I was so excited that I didn't really take the time to figure out how that was even possible. He certainly didn't know precisely how he was doing it."

Sara perked up and said, "Oh, your father was a Time Walker! How exciting! Those are quite rare, you know. It's a gene that can be passed down, so you might have it too."

At this, Lola slid sideways down the wall and hid her face in Sara's comforter. "Enough . . . I can't take any more! My brain is fried." she said, her voice muffled.

Sara came to kneel closer to her and tentatively ran her hand soothingly down Lola's back.

"There, there, love. It's a lot to take in, but you'll be alright. Why don't you go have a shower and get ready for bed? When you get back, you'll be right as rain. If you want to chat, we can talk about boys while I help you unpack. If not, we'll turn in early. How does that sound?" she asked in her chipper voice.

Lola lifted her head and replied, "Wonderful!" She got up and smoothed out Sara's bed with a pained expression. "Sorry about that. You really are a great roommate," she said as she got her toiletry bag, towel, and pajamas out of her trunk.

Sara waved her off again and added, "Go 'long with you! It's my pleasure, for sure. Now go to the showers before there's a queue a mile long!"

The shower was divine. When she got back to the room, Sara had put the bedspread Lola had brought from home on her bed and stacked her books neatly in the bookcase. Her side of the room already looked better. She apparently hadn't touched anything else, which was good because Lola wasn't used to people touching her stuff. She thanked her roommate and started putting what few things were left away. Then, she put away her uniform in the wardrobe. As she did so, the girls chatted about boys. Lola told Sara about Jackson. Sara told her about the boys in their year. Lola was disappointed when she didn't mention Devlin, but she was too shy to ask about him outright. She was quite fascinated by him and she felt a little disloyal to Jackson. It felt good to talk with a girlfriend about a regular topic. Time flew by and soon the lights were flickering. It was time for bed. Just before nodding off to sleep, Lola made a mental note to ask Sara again about all the girls having a name that ended with an *a*.

CHAPTER 7
MONDAY MORNING

LOLA WOKE UP CONFUSED. Where was she? For the second time in a month, she was waking up in a strange bed, in a strange room. This time, she was at The Academy, a magical school for kids with traveling keys taught by magical creatures in a magical world that didn't exist. All caught up.

She got up, went to the bathroom, washed her face, brushed her teeth, and went back to the room. It was early and Sara was still asleep. She had no phone or watch, so she went by the clock above the door. Rolling out her yoga mat, she sat to meditate for twenty minutes. Then, she went through a sequence of asanas that her aunt had taught her. Looking out the window, she saw the grounds came alive as the sun rose, though she couldn't see the sunrise. She decided this view would be even better with coffee. She got dressed and headed for the girls' Sitting Room to hunt for a cup of joe.

When she got there, she realized she wasn't the only early riser, nor was she the only coffee drinker. She also noted, gratefully, that none of the girls were chatting. In fact, they were all silent, waving their hellos and miming to pass the cream and such. Lola was really pleased about this as she hated talking before her morning coffee. As she approached the coffee machine, she saw there was a sign on the wall, written on parchment paper with what appeared to be a quill.

Dear Ladies,

We respectfully ask that you observe our total silence rule until 8 a.m. We are not morning people. Those of us who are up, don't necessarily want to chat. Some of us would like to sleep in as long as possible. If you are a chatty Cathy, please go down to breakfast where you can chat to your heart's content.

Yours,

The Girls

Lola sighed. She was among kindred spirits. She grabbed a cup, filled it with the timeless morning elixir, and went to stand by the window. Here, she could glimpse the sun at the far right. There was no situation that coffee and a sunrise couldn't make better. She drank her coffee in blissful silence, turning occasionally to wave at girls coming in as she heard the shuffling of feet. When she was done, she washed her cup, put it away, and went back to the room.

Sara was up and dressed, reclining on her made bed with her book. "There you are!" she exclaimed when Lola came in. She put away her book and got off the bed. "Are you ready for breakfast?" she asked.

Lola smiled. She liked that her new friend was so enthusiastic. She mostly liked that she had had a full hour to herself before having to interact with the chipper girl, or anyone else. God only knew what buffet-style breakfast was going to be like, but Lola was sure it was going to be loud.

She grabbed her satchel and her schedule. "I'm ready," she said, resolutely.

THEY WERE mid way down the staircase and Lola could hear the cacophony of the Dining Room. Lola and Sara went to their table and sat in the same seats as the day before. It seemed this would be her seat from now on. Lola was a little disappointed to note that Devlin had not come down yet. Or perhaps he had come and gone. It was now seven-fifteen.

The girls greeted the gang and helped themselves to the various beverages on the table. Another coffee and a glass of orange juice for Lola. Sara had tea and a glass of grapefruit juice. Then they went over to the buffet. It certainly rivaled anything that Phyllis and Marie had put together at the Mansion. There was everything anyone could possibly want for breakfast, no matter where they came from. Lola decided she would try something new every day, starting tomorrow. Today, she needed bacon and eggs. And a chocolate croissant. She loaded her plate and went back to the table. Only half of the table was having breakfast by now and everyone was concentrating on eating as they had to be in a class by eight-fifteen.

When they were done, Sara explained that they needed to put their dishes and cutlery in the bins on the far wall, but the glasses stayed on the tables. Once that task was complete, Sara took Lola to the Common Room as she hadn't been in there the night before, though she had seen it quickly during the tour. There, they found the rest of the gang, including Devlin. His face lit up when he saw Lola and she blushed profusely.

"I'm sorry I missed you at breakfast. What did you eat?" he asked with a wink.

Lola turned a deeper shade of red. *What was it with guys and food?* she wondered.

"Leave the poor lass alone, Devlin. She's having a hard enough time adjusting to all this without you harassing her," interjected Sara, putting a protective arm around Lola.

"Settle down, mama bear. I mean no disrespect. It's a compliment I wish to be giving the lady. She knows that, right?" he asked, looking at Lola expectantly.

Lola, who had been staring at the floor to tamper her blush, was forced to look up into those steel-blue eyes. *Lord, but he is beautiful,* she thought and stammered, "Yes, of course. It's no problem. I'm an only child, so I'm not used to teasing. It's refreshing!" She exclaimed this as enthusiastically as she could.

There was no time to discuss it further because the lights blinked—it was time for class.

SARA WALKED with Lola to her first class, stopping along the way to point out the other classrooms on Lola's morning schedule. They were indeed fairly accessible and close together. As Sara went into a classroom, Lola wondered if she would have to sit in a class with a group of 13-year-olds.

She braced herself and opened the door to room E-121. It was an average-sized classroom, but there were only six tables with two chairs each. Textbooks were positioned neatly in the center of each table. Upfront, there was the teacher's desk and, behind it, a regular blackboard. The board was flanked by two large picture windows framed with heavy navy velour curtains. To the right, a door led to what looked like the teacher's office. On the left wall was a series of hand-drawn posters depicting various artifacts, maps, and other historical or geographical data.

Lola was trying to decide where to sit. She looked at her watch; it was eight-twelve, but the room was empty. She was clearly in the right room for her *History of Magical Artifacts* class. She re-checked her schedule; the class was meant to begin at eight-fifteen.

She set her satchel on one of the front tables and tentatively walked over to the office door to see if the teacher was in there.

He was seated in an armchair in front of the fireplace, reading intently. Lola cleared her throat but got no reaction out of the man. He had that absent-minded professor look about him. His curly red hair was unruly, his spectacles had slipped to the end of his nose, and though he seemed neatly attired, he still looked a bit rumpled.

Lola knocked softly on the doorjamb and said, "Dr. McClary?"

He looked up, a little startled. Then, looking at the time on the clock on the mantle, he quickly rose. "Just a moment, miss. I'll be right with you," he said motioning for her to back into the classroom. Lola mumbled, "Okay," and went to sit at the table, alone.

Meanwhile, Dr. McClary grabbed his suit jacket from the back of the armchair and put it on. Checking his reflection in the mirror above the fireplace, he straightened his tie, checked his teeth, and nodded his approval.

He came out of his office just as a chime was heard. It was eight-fifteen. "Good morning, class," he said to the room as he entered. Then, seeing Lola by herself, he went to his desk and looked in his planner. His face took on an *Ah, yes* look as he looked back at Lola.

"You must be Miss Evers. Welcome to The Academy. It's your very first day, am I correct?" he asked as he made his way over to her. He had a thick Scottish accent, though his enunciation was quite clear. To Lola's ears, it sounded rather musical.

"Yes, sir," she replied wondering if she should stand.

He put out his hand for her to shake and said, "I'm Dr. McClary, but you already knew that." He chuckled. "Your situation is a little different, though not unique." As if on cue, the classroom door opened, and Devlin entered.

"I apologize for my tardiness, Dr. McClary. I have a note from the Headmaster," said Devlin as he strode briskly down the row of desks to deliver the scroll. The teacher took it and read it. Devlin stood ramrod in front of him, at least a good head taller. Dr. McClary was nodding as he read. He rolled up the scroll and put it on his desk.

"As I was saying, your situation, Miss Evers, is not unique. Mr. Johansson here is also new to the school. Have you met?" asked the professor.

"Yes," they both answered at the same time and stopped to let the other answer. This seemed to be a satisfactory answer for the teacher, and he motioned for Devlin to sit at the table on the right. Lola and Devlin smiled quickly at one another then faced the teacher, awaiting instructions.

"This class is called *History of Magical Artifacts*. It is the third in a series of summer classes. The first being *History of Magic*, and the second being *History of Magical Worlds*. You will need to complete all three in the following two weeks. That is why there are only two of you. Should you require extra time, you may continue your studies independently at home, so long as you have completed your assignments by the fall term. The series is a prerequisite to the University Curriculum and since you'll be spending the fall term completing your high school degrees, you'll have no time to devote to it," explained the teacher.

He walked over to his desk and took two leather-bound notebooks. He handed one to each of them. Lola thanked him as she took hers and placed it on her desk. The words *The Academy* were embossed at the top. Her full name was embossed on the bottom—Lola Simone Evers. Impressed, she ran her fingers over the letters of her name.

"These are your planners. You'll only get one, so keep them safe and keep them neat. If you open them, you'll find they have a removable interior. Planners run from July to June. About a week before each term, your schedule will automatically populate," said Dr. McClary, walking to and fro in front of their tables, as though lecturing to a full class. *He's done this before*, thought Lola as she flipped to today's date and was nonetheless astonished to see all her classes had been filled out. She grinned and flipped to the following week and found those filled in as well. "This is so cool!" she whispered to herself.

The teacher kept his pace as he continued, "You were provided with a list of rules. They are conveniently repeated on page four of the planner, along with the list of clothing items you were provided. Be sure to leave those items in your Dormitory when you leave next week and to have any soiled items laundered so they are ready upon your return."

He paused his pacing and looked at them. "Do you have notebooks?" he asked. They both nodded and took them out of their bags. "Let us begin," he said as he resumed his pacing.

"You will have noticed that all the students at The Academy are humans. I should rather say most students. Some students are half-human," he amended. Lola was itching to ask what their other half might be, but she was sure he would cover that soon enough.

"The Faculty, however, is not. In fact, Dr. Thompson and I are the only human professors at The Academy. It's quite an honor. Should you like to know more about our journeys here, you'll find our memoirs in the library. Details on the various types of magical beings present here at school will be covered in the *Magical Communities* class I believe you are registered for. I shall defer to Sir Kravchuk."

Both Lola and Devlin were taking notes and listening attentively. The teacher took the top textbook from the pile on Lola's table and handed it to her. Devlin took his own book.

"Go to the illustration on page thirteen. This chart presents the various magical lineages with regards to humans. At this school, you'll find no Witches, Wizards, or Warlocks. There are other schools for them. Though you will have herbology classes at The Academy, please don't expect to produce any magical potions. You will be taught the healing arts through *Herbology*. And even though you will be taught *Latin for Incantations*, don't expect elaborate spellcasting," said the professor.

Lola's face fell. She could just imagine herself waving a magic wand and manifesting a stuffed-crust pepperoni pizza. Then, she thought back to the incantations her dad had used from the Archives and wondered if those were considered spellcasting. She'd be sure to ask Dr. Thompson in the next class.

"What kind of magical humans do we have here at The Academy? First, obviously, are the Travelers. Representing about seventy-five percent of the student body, Travelers are those who possess a key and can travel within the known world. Second are the Time Walkers, those who may travel within the known world in any timeline they chose. They represent about twenty percent of the student body. Third, are the World Jumpers. A very rare gift, five percent of the student body can travel within the known world as well and as to other worlds. The very skilled create worlds such as the one we are in. A skill only possessed, thus far, by High Elves."

Lola was writing furiously in her notebook and trying not to hyperventilate. A chime rang to signify the end of the class. Dr. McClary asked them to read the first five chapters before their next class and dismissed them. Lola took note of it in her new planner, put her things in her satchel, and headed for her next class.

CHAPTER 8

COURSE LOAD

LOLA HAD a similar experience in her second class. The classroom was identical, as was the teacher's office, though Dr. Thompson, an Englishman, was much neater in both appearance and decor. He was a man of average height, with short, well-groomed brown hair, and piercing brown eyes. The kind of eyes that would miss nothing. His three-piece suit was perfectly pressed, though a little boring. He had a cheerful manner, but Lola could tell he would be firm and demanding. He had already written notes on the blackboard.

As they introduced themselves, Devlin came in. It would seem they were a matched pair for the Summer Program. For the theoretical classes, anyhow. The good news was that Lola had no time for blushing or overthinking because there was so much information to absorb. It kept her mind on safe topics. She liked school, in general. And the topics presented, though a little heavy for summer break, were interesting. This class would be easy. Lola had never taken Latin, but she had taken Spanish for three years and languages came easily to her.

They sat in their respective seats and the teacher began. He too announced that this class was the third in a series of classes they would need to master before the fall term. The first class was *Latin Basics*, the second was called *Advanced Latin*, and the third *Latin for*

Incantations. All three textbooks were on the tables and the information on the blackboard was the outline for the first class as well as their assignment. It seems Lola was not going to have much free time in the evenings and she now had plans for Saturday as well as Sunday morning.

Soon enough the chime rang and it was time to move on to the next class. Instead of going their separate ways, Devlin and Lola checked their schedules and confirmed they were together in the next two classes. They agreed they might as well stick together.

As THEY ENTERED yet another identical classroom, they were surprised to see their teacher, Sir Kravchuk, seated on his desk, smoking a pipe that emitted no smoke while staring at the ceiling intently. *He must be deep in thought.* She blushed when she remembered how she had fainted when she first saw him at orientation. She really hadn't gotten that good of a look at him. Though she had since been told he was a Goblin, he was the size of a Dwarf, or a person of short stature if you were trying to be politically correct.

However, his head seemed somewhat more proportional to the rest of his body. His distinctive features were the hooked nose and long pointy ears. Contrary to what Lola had read, his skin was not green, though it was a shade darker than hers. Whether this was his natural skin color or the result of exposure to the sun, Lola had no idea but was looking forward to finding out.

They walked slowly toward his desk, so as not to catch him off guard. They both seemed a little wary. When they stood beside the first row of desks Devlin spoke up to get his attention.

"Good morning, Sir Kravchuk. We are Lola and Devlin. Pleased to make your acquaintance," he said with some reverence. Lola wondered if she should curtsy. He was called *sir* after all.

His eyes snapped to them instantly and he seemed to scowl at them initially. He looked at each of them, from head to toe, for a good long while. His gaze was so intense that Lola was beginning to squirm under his scrutiny. He turned and deposited his pipe in a bowl on his desk and got down using a three-step wooden box on the side of the desk. He came around and poked Lola's stomach. He was eye-level with it.

When Lola jumped, he asked, "Are you going to faint again?" His stout little body was shaking with laughter and he slapped his hand on his thigh. Devlin looked at her inquiringly, but she didn't reply. She wondered if she should laugh too, or cry, or flee, or even feign another fainting episode. Her hands were gripping the end of her blazer.

"I apologize, sir. I meant no disrespect. I'd never seen anyone who wasn't . . . human before," she said diplomatically.

His face grew more serious and a kind, grandfatherly smile appeared on his lips.

"Don't you worry about that. I was just teasing. I was also trying to make a point. It's uncomfortable to be stared at, though it's perfectly normal to be curious," he said shaking a finger. He walked over to Devlin and poked him in the thigh, then went back to sitting upon his desk.

"That is why the study of *Magical Communities* is on the curriculum for our new arrivals, though they are usually much younger than the two of you. Once we've completed the curriculum for this class, we'll move on to the next and final level," he said as he sat back on his chair.

Lola glanced at the table to her left and saw two identical textbooks —Levels 1 and 2. Devlin shifted from one foot to another. This prompted the teacher to invite them to sit down and take out a note-book. He then waved backward at the blackboard and it filled with text in neat cursive. Lola's lips parted into an *O* but she made no sound. Devlin uttered a loud, "Wow." Sir Kravchuk only chuckled and began his lecture.

"*Magical Communities* refers to humanoid species of non-celestial beings that have magical abilities or predispositions. This includes human sub-species such as Wizards, Warlocks, Witches, and other types of magicians. We will not cover them in this class as information is readily available on your Internet. We will also not cover the species that attend this school as that will be covered in Dr. McClary's class. Level 1 of this class will, therefore, cover general knowledge on Dwarfs, Goblins, Gnomes, Elves—think of the Keebler Elves, High Elves—think of the Elves from Lord of the Rings, Fairies, Pixies, Mermaids, Sirens, and Valkyries. Level 2 of this class teaches how to interact positively with each of the species."

Both Lola and Devlin were taking notes. When they seemed to have finished what he'd already written on the board, he waved his hand again to produce more notes after those. He lectured until the chime sounded and gave them their assignment before dismissing them.

Lola was starting to run out of steam. Her hand hurt from taking so many notes and she was starting to feel overwhelmed by all the home-work she'd have to do. Devlin walked quietly beside her as they headed to their last class of the morning. Then, just before they entered the classroom, he touched her arm lightly to get her attention.

"Chin up, only one more before lunch!" he said with a wink.

Lola was too tired to laugh, but she smiled. "Yeah, but look at all the homework we have! How are we supposed to get through all of this before the next class?" she asked.

"If you like, we can work together in the library after dinner. To save time, we could read the chapters for different classes, take notes and share our notes," he suggested optimistically.

Lola's face lit up. "That's a brilliant idea. Then, when we have more time, we can re-read those chapters, so it sinks in," she said enthusias-tically.

Devlin smiled and nodded his agreement. He opened the door and motioned for her to enter the classroom. If Devlin had lifted her spirits with his encouraging words, the sight before her made Lola's heart sing. The classroom, though identical to the others from the outside, held quite the surprise on the inside. There were the same two rows of desks, teacher's desk, and office, but behind the teacher's desk, instead of a blackboard flanked by picture windows, were two French doors leading out to a huge greenhouse. The teacher was nowhere to be seen, but one of the French doors was ajar. They dropped their bags on the tables and went in search of their Herbology professor.

As they entered, Lola was hit first by the smell. A fragrant cross between fresh rain, wet dirt, and unnamed flowers. It was wonderful. Devlin seemed to be appreciating it as well because he kept taking deep breaths and sighing. Lola did the same and she felt all the stress drain from her body. They walked slowly down the main aisle in a complete, fascinated daze. As far as Lola was concerned, she didn't recognize any of the plants she saw. But they were beautiful. The colors were so vibrant and unusual; blue petals on a type of daisy, an orange tree that produced bright green fruit—there was even purple ground cover. Devlin kept point at things and telling her to look and she was doing the same. The plants had nameplates written in Latin. Lola deduced that they would put their lessons into practice sooner rather than later.

As they reached the end of the aisle, there was another set of French doors, leading outside. In front of them stood a long table with what looked like a small-scale model of the school. Lola marveled at the beauty of the construction, though she couldn't tell if it was a good likeness as she had not been outside yet. It was great to get her bearings, though. It didn't have a dome, but there was a clear plexiglass *fence* around the property. There were many footpaths, but no roads. Which made sense as the roads would lead nowhere. Devlin was walking around the table, looking closely and grinning.

"This is amazing. Look, they even have a pink bee flying about," he said pointing at a pink dot hovering over some shrubs near the Main Entrance. Lola was only half listening because she too had caught movement. In the Greenhouse. She could see something blue and red.

"No!" she yelled incredulously. "Devlin, could you turn around and wave your hand to someone outside?" she asked.

Devlin turned around and was starting to wave but saw no one.

"There's no one out there," he said in confusion.

"Humor me," was Lola's reply.

Reluctantly, Devlin waved his arm in greeting to the invisible someone.

Lola shrieked. "What?" he asked, running back to her side of the table.

Lola was pointing a shaky finger at the Greenhouse. "What?" asked Devlin again. "Did you see a snake?" he tried.

"It's not a model, it's some sort of mirror image. That's us in the Greenhouse. When you waved, I saw you through the glass!" said Lola breathlessly.

Devlin started to laugh, but Lola's expression sobered him quickly. He bent down to look closer. He obviously couldn't see himself in front of the door as he'd was now on the other side of the table. Just then, as they were peering intently trying to catch a glimpse of themselves, the pink bee hovered in front of the Greenhouse door. They looked at each other, then straightened up to look out the actual door. Something was hovering there alright. And it was pink, but it wasn't a bee. It was morphing into Professor Elderberry! Her feet touched the ground in a graceful landing, and she opened the door.

"Hello, children. Welcome to *Herbology*!" she said with a dazzling smile.

Then all faded to black.

CHAPTER 9

MAGIC

LOLA WAS DREAMING. She was flying on a magic carpet over a field of lavender. She reached to pluck a flower and brought it to her nose, but the smell was foul, and the flower was talking to her.

"Lola, wake up!" said the flower.

Her eyelids fluttered a few times and she thought she opened her eyes. Cinderella was kneeling beside her waving a green foul-smelling flower in front of her face. She waved it away and closed her eyes, wanting to go back to the magic carpet.

"Lola!" said a voice that was not Cinderella's. It was a man that sounded familiar, but she couldn't place it. Then someone pressed something cool on her forehead and stroked her head. "Phyllis, is that you?" she asked dreamily.

"No, it's Devlin. You need to wake up now," the voice said.

Devlin? Lola was confused. What was he doing in her dream? Then she remembered and her eyes flew open.

"Easy now," said Cinderella, or rather Professor Elderberry it seemed. "We haven't had a fainter in years, how delightful!" she exclaimed happily though she didn't seem to be making fun of Lola.

Lola squinted at her. "You were a bee. You were flying outside!" she accused her.

"Yes, dear. I can fly inside as well but it's a little cramped in here," replied the professor.

Devlin laughed at this, but Lola wasn't so sure. She started to get up, but both the professor and Devlin took her arms and eased her gently up, so she wouldn't be dizzy.

"Um, thanks. I apologize for fainting," said Lola lamely. That's when she noticed she had been lying down on the first-row table in the classroom. She scooted down from the table, brushed down her uniform, and stuck out her hand.

"Hello, Professor Elderberry, I'm Lola Evers," she said.

The teacher shook her hand and put her other hand on Lola's shoulder and replied, "Pleased to meet you, Lola. Please, call me Petunia. I just know we'll be great friends."

Lola smiled and took her seat. Devlin did the same. They were ready to begin.

"As I said before, welcome to *Herbology*. I'm sure by now you've been told you have a lot of catching up to do," said the teacher, hands clasped behind her back as she stood in front of her desk. Lola took in her magical appearance. She wore a lovely pink chiffon dress that would have been more suited to a lady's lunch. Her hair was swept up in an elaborate updo that comprised a long, loose blond braid entwined with dried sprigs and wound in a spiral atop her head. She really did look like a fairy princess.

"You may also be wondering why the class is not part of the afternoon curriculum," she continued. "It's quite simple. I find that studying plants from books is neither efficient nor enjoyable! You have to see a plant, smell it, and feel it, to really know it. And you must know it well before you can do anything with it," she said with great fervor.

"Take out your notebooks." She waited for them to be ready and continued, "There are two *Herbology* classes offered in the summer program. The first is known as *Entry to Herbology*; it covers the basics of plant identification and properties. The second is *Herbology for Wellness* and explains how to use herbs in daily life. *Herbology for Healing* is only offered at the university level."

She took out a small wand from her pocket and tapped the air in front of Lola and Devlin.

A scroll appeared in front of each of them, suspended in mid-air at eye-level.

"These are your assignments, write them down," she instructed patiently.

They heard the chime and hurriedly wrote down the information in their planners and Devlin exclaimed, "Lunch!" Lola laughed while she grabbed a textbook and put her things away in her bag. It was getting heavy!

Devlin was waiting for her by the door. She turned to the professor and said, "Thanks for your help, Professor Elderberry. See you tomorrow!" and went to join Devlin.

"Call me Petunia!" called out the teacher as she waved at them. "And if you want to help out or just take a break, the Greenhouse is open to students from six-thirty to seven-thirty in the morning."

Lola smiled and replied, "Thanks, I'll keep that in mind!" as she exited the room.

"I WAS MORTIFIED," she told Sara and the group about her fainting, yet again, at lunch. No sense in trying to keep it a secret; she was sure it would get out soon enough. Everyone laughed good-naturedly.

The conversation died as soon as the food was served. Everyone was famished, including Lola. On today's menu was a huge green salad with a choice of three dressings, a hot cauldron of seafood chowder, lemon and herb roasted chicken drumsticks, and sweet potato fries. For dessert, there were custard jars and assorted shortbread cookies. At lunch, coffee and tea carafes were placed on the tables along with the water pitchers.

Plates were passed around and soon everyone was eating joyfully. Eventually, the volume around the room rose as teenagers chatted excitedly about their first day of classes. Lola realized she'd spent the morning with Devlin but hadn't so much as exchanged a few words with him. She had been completely absorbed by the classes, the teachers, and, well, the magic. She cast a sideways look at him. He was chatting with Colin and James, trying to get them to understand that their combined names were that of a singer. It was obvious why Sara had asked if he had fallen from heaven. He looked like a cherub with all that curly blond hair and fair skin. *Maybe one of his parents was an angel.*

She looked around at the other tables to see if anyone else stood out as much as he did. When no one caught her eye, she wondered if the only reason he stood out so much was that she liked him. Maybe the glow that came off his skin was all in her imagination. She leaned closer to Sara and whispered, "Do you think Devlin is part angel?"

Sara burst out laughing and caught everyone's attention. Lola made eyes at her to keep quiet. But Lenora and Clara were asking what was so funny. Sara winked at Lola conspiratorially and then exclaimed, "Lola just realized all the girl names at the table finish with an *a*."

Lenora's brows knit together, and she replied, "That's true, but why is it so funny?"

"Because she asked me about it last night and I was going to explain when we got to the room but we got so caught up talking about boys, it completely slipped my mind!" she lied smoothly.

Lola's eyes widened as she realized she had forgotten to ask Sara about it.

They were saved from more probing questions when Devlin put in, "Hey, that's true! Why do your names all end with an *a*? Is it all girls at the school or just the ones at this table?" He had asked this of no one in particular.

The girls looked at one another as though to decide who would field this question for the newbies. They seem to settle on Lenora.

"Well, now. It's an ancient custom. Back when magic was a household name, giving females a name ending with an *a* helped identify those with magic," she explained.

"But what if someone called their non-magical child Glenda?" Lola asked.

"They would never do that back in the day. It was an accepted fact," replied Lenora.

"But what about the boys?" asked Devlin.

"Magical ability is passed through the mother. Therefore, if a boy's mother had an *a* at the end of their name, then it was assumed he had the magical ability as well," she said.

Lola was mulling this over. It seemed far-fetched.

"But my mother had no magical abilities and I only recently found out it came from my dad. I'm pretty sure she chose my name and it had nothing to do with that custom," she said.

"That may be true. But it's quite a coincidence, don't you think?" replied Sara.

The lights blinked, indicating the end of lunch. Lola decided to investigate this further when she had some free time.

CHAPTER 10
PRACTICAL MAGIC

LOLA AND SARA went back to the room to drop off and empty their book bags and get their afternoon stuff. The monogrammed laundry bag doubled nicely as a gym bag. Though Lola usually wore her hair loose, she decided to braid it just in case the afternoon's activities required it. She had *Traveling* class first, then *Martial Arts*. It was a relief not to have anything strenuous right after lunch since she was stuffed.

They quickly went back down to wait for their teachers in the Main Hall. Sara asked about her morning classes and Lola explained about the semi-private lessons and the enormous course load. Sara groaned in sympathy for her friend and told her nothing too interesting went on at night during the Summer Program except for the odd campfire where they made s'mores. Most of the activities were aimed to keep the younger kids busy and out of trouble—like board games, treasures hunts, and various team sports. They weren't used to spending so much time away from screens and devices, and the boys had a lot of energy.

The Hall was filling with students and Sara had to raise her voice a little to ask about Devlin. Lola had nothing to share. She hoped to get a chance to get to know him as the days went by. But she did tell Sara about their prospective study dates.

"Well, that's promising! A couple of book nerds flirting in the Library after dark," said Sara, looking off into space as though imagining the scene. Lola nudged her with her shoulder.

"Stop that!" she said, then grew still as the lights flickered and everyone grew quiet.

The teachers showed up and, one by one, they invited the students to follow them. The *Martial Arts* and *Mindfulness and Meditation classes* were led outdoors, whereas *Traveling* and *Magic* classes were in the west wing. She and Devlin followed Lady Samsara to the classroom. As they walked, she told them they could meet her there directly tomorrow as they were old enough to be trusted alone in the west wing. Lola thought that was a peculiar statement but hesitated to ask for further information. Devlin had no qualms at all and quickly asked, "What do you mean, Lady Samsara?"

"Students are not allowed in the west wing in the summer without adult supervision. The classrooms contain certain volatile components that could lead to injury in novice hands," she explained. Now Lola was even more curious. That seemed cryptic and dangerous. *What was going on in the west wing?* she wondered.

Their teacher was very graceful; she seemed to glide down the Hall, her long flowing robe hugging the floor as she went. She had very long silvery-white hair tied back with a silver chain attached to a thin silver headpiece with a silver-blue stone over the third eye. She wore no other adornments.

Her skin was pale and papery thin. Lola could see no signs of age, but she had the distinct impression that the Lady was older than she looked.

As they arrived in the west wing, Lola tried to see into the classrooms, but most doors had no windows and those that did were frosted. There were a lot of doors here. Lola was about to ask what other classes were taught here when Lady Samsara beat her to it.

"These rooms are used mainly during the school year for the

university classes you'll be taking in the fall," she said and stopped before a door marked only with W-155. She took out an ancient key and unlocked the door. As she did, she spoke some words too softly for Lola to hear but it was obvious that it was a spell or passphrase of some sort.

The door opened onto a very large room, divided by a floor to ceiling glass partition. On one side was the standard classroom set-up with long tables, a teacher's desk, and a blackboard. The other was empty though Lola could see numbered green dots on the floor at regular intervals.

Lady Samsara led them to the classroom, and they settled in their usual seats. Both took out a notebook and a pen and were poised to begin their notetaking. *Model pupils*, she thought wryly.

The teacher went to her desk and retrieved two small books and gave them each a print. The leather-bound copies were embossed with their names and were titled *The Traveler's Handbook.*

"If you had followed the usual course of things, you would have received this four years ago and you would know it by heart. Memorize it; you *will* be tested," she said sternly.

"Open your books to *Chapter 1, Preparing to travel*. Which of you has already traveled alone thus far?" she asked. Peering closer at them she added, "I see you are both wearing your keys, so I assume that you have."

Only Lola raised her hand. Devlin looked at her, astonished. The teacher asked how she came about getting a key and what instructions she had received. When Lola explained about her mother, moving to Williamsburg, Phyllis's instructions, and the Evers family history, the teacher looked appalled. Lola was happy she had not mentioned her time-traveling dad, the council, and the incantations. There was time enough to disclose those facts later.

"Where did you go on your own?" she asked, curious.

This was getting complicated, thought Lola. She didn't want to lie but there was no way to tell the truth without telling the whole story.

"I went to a beach in Hawaii for a few minutes," she said finally. It wasn't a lie, she had gone there, but with Phyllis.

Lips pursed in concentration, Lady Samsara looked at her intently, the way her mother had when she doubted Lola was telling the truth, but she didn't press the matter. She turned to Devlin and asked him about his key. Devlin was still staring at Lola, open-mouthed. He jumped a little when Lady Samsara repeated her question.

"Yes . . . I was raised by my mother. I never knew my father. Mother said he died before I was born. A few weeks ago, my mother was in a car accident and was killed instantly. Since I was about to turn eighteen, the *Polisen* said I could stay in our home without a guardian, though they assigned a caseworker to come to check on me twice a week. When the barrister came on my birthday, he said mother had left a little money for me but that I would need to get a job if I wanted to continue living in our townhouse, otherwise it would need to be sold. Then he said Mother had given him some things to give me when I turned eighteen. He gave me a letter and a small, intricately carved wooden box. When I went to open it, he said I should wait until I was alone. He gave me a piece of paper that held the combination to the tiny lock I hadn't noticed. He explained that my mother had never opened it because there was no key. But the combination to the lock had been tucked into the felt underside of the box. He wished me good luck, gave me his card, and bade me farewell," he said.

Though she wanted to say she was sorry for his loss when Lola opened her mouth something else entirely came out.

"What was in the box?" she asked, though she was pretty sure she already knew.

He seemed relieved for some reason and answered her question.

"There was a key as well as a small iridescent marble," he said.

"A marble?" she asked, her face scrunching up in confusion. "I didn't get a marble," she said looking from Devlin to Lady Samsara who was nodding knowingly.

"We can save the marble for later. Suffice it to say that it means Devlin is a World Jumper," she stated.

Both Devlin and Lola wore identical flabbergasted looks. Neither of them had had time to read the assigned chapters in the *History of Magic* textbook, but now they were burning to read it cover to cover.

"I can see you have many questions, most of which will be answered when you crack open your textbooks. For now, let's begin with the basics," she said. Then she added, "Lola, go back to the inside cover of the Handbook and please read the disclaimer for us." She moved behind her desk and sat down.

Lola opened the Handbook to the inside cover and began reading aloud.

"Traveling, like driving a motor vehicle, is a skill that requires knowledge and practice to ensure the safety of all involved. Traveling without a license, so to speak, can lead to untold catastrophes and even to injury and death."

"Mr. Johansson, could you tell us what happened when you took the key out of the box?" the teacher asked him.

Devlin blushed and raked his fingers through his hair. "A door appeared out of nowhere," he said emphatically.

Lola laughed, remembering her own astonishment. Then she sobered as she realized he had been alone with no one to guide him. "I'm sorry. That was insensitive. You must have been frightened," she said contritely.

"Well, I fell off my chair! Then I put the key back in the box and reached for the letter, which I should have done first. Isn't that what parents tell us, read the card before you open the gift?" he said ruefully.

"What did the letter say?" asked Lola fascinated by his story.

"It was from Mother, explaining that the box had appeared out of nowhere one day when I was about thirteen years old. It had no postmark, so someone must have broken in to deliver it while we were out. The box was engraved with my name. She had tried to open the box but found no key. She took it into her room so I wouldn't see it. For days, she said she stared at the box, unable to decide what to do. My mother comes from a very superstitious family and she said the box made her nervous, like it had evil energy inside. In the end, she gave it to the barrister for safekeeping. She wrote that it was now up to me to figure out what was inside," he said solemnly.

"Then what happened?" asked Lola, hanging on his every word.

Lady Samsara was now perched on the side of her desk, listening intently.

"I put everything back in the box and went to take a shower to clear my head. When I came back out, another letter lay on the kitchen table. It had not been there before; I was sure of it. I checked the doors and windows, but everything was secure. I opened the letter and it was an admission letter to the Academy, inviting me, with instructions, to the Orientation. The rest, as they say, is history," he concluded.

Lady Samsara got up and approached their desks. "I'm very sorry for both your losses. I hope you'll consider those at The Academy like a second family and a home whenever you need it," she said simply.

Devlin nodded stiffly and flipped the pages in the Handbook uncomfortably.

"Alright, children, follow me," she said as she went to the door leading to the other side of the glass partition. "When children arrive here for the first time at thirteen years of age, they have not received their keys, or marbles, as it were. Though most of them have seen their family members use them, and some have traveled along. They are eager to begin, as you can imagine." She opened the door and let them in before her. "Here is where they have their first experience. In a secure environment, where they learn to focus and act responsibly. This room will let you travel—only within it, from one dot to another. Later, I can make it so you can travel within the school, then the dome," she explained.

She motioned for them to each stand on a dot and take notice of the way they were numbered. Then she had Lola take out her key. When the door appeared, she asked her to think of home and try the door. It was impossible. Then she asked her to think of number twenty-five and see the green dot in her mind's eye. Lola did so. When she opened the door, an identical door appeared in front of the number twenty-five dot. She put her arm through and waved it about. Her hand was immediately seen coming out of the other door. She yanked it out and put her hands to her face in shock. "O.M.G.," was all she could muster.

"Go through it! Go through it!" said Devlin excitedly.

Lady Samsara laughed despite herself. "You are no better than the 13-year-olds," she chided. "Perhaps you should join their group," she suggested.

Both Lola and Devlin gave her a look that said what they both thought of that idea.

"All right then, go through it," she encouraged.

Lola went through it but didn't close the door. Devlin was jumping up and down yelling, "You're over there!"

The door she had used to depart was still completely visible, as was the one she had arrived through. The teacher told her to close the door. She did, and both doors disappeared.

"That is so cool," then turning to Devlin, she said, "You try!" After which she quickly added, "If Lady Samsara agrees, of course."

"Yes, of course. Devlin, take out your key. Picture the green dot in your mind and go to number fifteen," she advised.

Devlin took out his key. It was attached to a chain and came out of his pants pocket. As he produced the key, a red door appeared.

"Why does he have a red door?" asked Lola. "Is there a significance to the color door that shows up?"

"There is, and it's covered in the Handbook, but it's irrelevant at this moment."

Devlin thought of green dot number fifteen and opened the door. They saw his door appear across the room and they were astonished all over again. Instead of waving a hand, he struck out his long leg through the door. Lola giggled and shouted, "Go through it! Go through it," the way he had. He went through the door, looked back at the door he had started from, shook his head in amazement, and closed the door.

The teacher had them practice a few more times before they returned to class. Lola was thinking this would be a very cool parlor trick, a fast way to get from one room to the next. She couldn't wait to try it at home and scare poor Phyllis!

They were both red-cheeked and breathless when they came back. The teacher gave them their assignment, "Read the entire Handbook and write down any questions you may have."

The chime sounded and she reminded them to come straight down the next day, as she would be waiting for them.

They left the room and talked about the experience with great animation. As they got to the hall, he asked if they were still on to study at the library after dinner. She agreed and they both went to change for *Martial Arts*.

CHAPTER II
MARTIAL ARTS

LOLA WAITED with her new friends in the Main Hall. Sara explained that for the last afternoon class, the students were divided by skill and not age. She and the others left with Professor Brambles for the *Advanced Mindfulness and Meditation* class.

When Master Smoke came to gather his group of students, Lola was surprised to be among a very large group of pupils. Indeed, more than half of the student population of the school followed him out into the courtyard. It was Lola's first time outside the school. She breathed in the air and held her face to the sun. The air smelled like fresh-cut grass. Lola opened her eyes and wondered if they had created an actual sun for this world or if it was all illusion. *Would I tan or burn if I stayed out for too long?*

Master Smoke asked the students to form into three lines and pointed to where he wanted each group: new students, White belts, and Blue belts. Each line started from the stone semi-circle in front of the Main Hall door and followed the angle of the lines in the stone. The first student stood on the grass behind his designated line, the next put a hand on his right shoulder, arms straight to measure the distance and the next student did the same until each student was in a line and the lines fanned out into four arcs. Lola went to stand with the new students. As she looked around, a boy standing in the Blue belt line was staring and smiling at her. She smiled at him and went to the back of the line. As she looked over at the last student of the next line, they were at least fifty feet apart.

Master Smoke went to the front of the line of the Blue belts. He faced the first student, put a hand on his left shoulder, and spoke words in a language Lola could not understand. He released his grip, clapped his hands and said something like *Hop*. The students did an about-face and started walking towards a red Japanese mini temple that hadn't been there seconds ago. They filed in and the doors closed.

Lola peered at the other students in her line, looking for Devlin. The younger students ahead of her were as surprised as she was. She turned to look behind her and found Devlin, grinning like a hyena a few spots back. When she heard the teacher say *Hop* again, she swiftly turned and looked ahead. He was sending the White belts to their very own little temple.

As he faced the new students, Lola thought his face held a hint of a smile. The group did an about-face and headed for the structure. It was an empty space except for some cushions on the floor in a circle around the room. She and the other students filed in and went to stand in front of a cushion but didn't sit down. There were fourteen of them and fourteen cushions.

The teacher entered and closed the doors. He stood before them, put his hands together as though in prayer mode and bowed to them. They all did the same. He walked around the room and looked at each of them in turn, mumbling to himself occasionally. When he returned to his spot, he addressed them with a heavily accented English.

"Welcome to *Martial Arts* class. I am Master Smoke. In this class, you will learn self-defense basics roughly based on Brazilian Jiu-Jitsu. It provides the opportunity for the development of an embodied spirituality by seeking divine blessing in three ways. Firstly, it provides an opportunity to gain respect for your physical gifts and limitations. Secondly, the pursuit of, and engagement in, a state of flow leads to the cultivation of virtue. Thirdly, the chief virtue that can be cultivated is that of humility, as Brazilian Jiu-Jitsu is both a competitive and collaborative sport," he explained.

"Raise your hand if you have studied Brazilian Jiu-Jitsu before," he said. Five students raised their hands, including Devlin. "Show me," said the master. He called the first student to the center. They sparred for less than two minutes. The master backed-up and bowed, and the student bowed in response. "Blue," he said and pointed at the door. The student bowed again and left quickly. Devlin was next, he too was sent to Blue. It was the same for the next four students. They were all sent to White.

When the last of them had gone, he motioned for the remaining students to sit down. Instinctively, most students sat cross-legged, some in half-lotus and others in full lotus. Master did not comment, he only nodded. Then he put his hands on his knees and closed his eyes. The students did the same. Lola figured they were going to meditate first, to relax. She certainly needed to relax. They were sitting in a temple that had appeared out of thin air. And questions like who was teaching the other groups were running through her mind. She needed to calm her mind. She inhaled slowly, counting to five, then exhaled, counting to five. Eventually, she forgot where she was and sat in total bliss.

"The ability to relax is very important. If you train without the ability to relax, sooner or later you will become exhausted, and more likely than not, injured. A tense, competitive mindset slows your progress. Students learn fastest when they are relaxed. It is easier said than done. Professor Brambles, the *Mindfulness and Meditation* teacher, will help you with that." She heard the master talking and assumed it was okay to open her eyes. She looked around and the other students were looking at and listening to Master Smoke attentively.

"In Jiu-Jitsu, you will learn the *Basics*, the *Fundamentals*, and the *Concepts*. *Basics* are the core of individual techniques that are simpler in their execution. *Fundamentals* are not so much specific techniques as they are practices and habits that are behind the execution of the techniques," he explained.

"Base, posture, pressure, ability to move the hips, managing distance, and using frames are all examples of *Fundamentals*," he went on. "There are six concepts: One—Position before submission. Two—Control your opponent. Three—Maintain good posture. Four—Stay relaxed. Five—Prevent your opponent from posting. Six—Look for opportunities to create mismatches," he said.

"As you can see, there are two concepts you can already work on, staying relaxed and posture. I will let Professor Brambles guide you in the proper seated posture. Please rise so we may work on your standing posture," he requested.

As they stood, a murmur of astonished whispers went around the room. All the students were now wearing white kimonos and a white belt. They all had the same reaction, patting themselves down, wondering how this was happening. Master Smoke said something that sounded like *Hut* and everyone came to attention. He demonstrated the standing position he expected them to have. Feet hip-distance apart, toes spread out, legs straight, tummy in, back straight, looking straight ahead, arms out a few inches in front of your thighs, fists closed but relaxed, shoulders back and straight, yet relaxed. He inspected each student and corrected when necessary. He went back to sit down but motioned for them to remain standing.

"As you rise from a seated position, this is how you should stand. Let me demonstrate first then I'll explain it in detail as I do it a second time," he said then got up and sat back down again.

"First, sit on the ground with your knees bent and your feet on the floor. Then, lean to one side so that one hip and the side of the same leg are on the ground. Put that same side's hand firmly on the ground a little behind and to the right of your hip. For instance, assuming you sit to the right, your right hand will be behind you and the outside of your right leg will be on the ground." He paused and motioned for them to try it.

"Next, post your left foot squarely on the ground with your knee bent. You will be putting all your weight on this foot and your posted right hand. Try this. Lift your right leg and seat off the ground as you balance on your left foot and your right hand. But then put everything back on the ground for now." He stopped to check on the students.

"Next, protect your head by grabbing the back of it with your free left hand, keeping your elbow close to your face. Doing so will bring your arm to your face in a way that will protect it from blows your opponent or attacker might try to inflict," he said, then went around the room to adjust a few students.

"Now it's time to get up. Again, place all your weight on your right hand and left foot. Lift your right hip and leg, and your seat off the ground. At this point, in self-defense or MMA situations, you could move your right hip forward to kick at the leg of your opponent or attacker with the leg you lifted off the ground," he continued and demonstrated it before checking on the students.

"Next, bring your right leg back and plant your right foot on the ground BEHIND your right hand, which should stay posted on the ground. You want to establish a wide base where your feet are firmly planted a bit farther than hip-distance apart. A narrow base, when your feet are close together, is less stable," he explained and took another break to go around the room.

"Your left arm should continue to protect your head and face as you lift your right hand off the ground and end up in an upright position, though you should keep your knees bent and your hips down. Notice that as you stand up, you will be standing up AWAY from the other person, placing much, but not all, of your weight on your rear right foot, which puts you in a position either to engage, in a sport situation or to run away, in a self-defense situation. This is much more preferable to leading with your face, standing up into your opponent or attacker, and otherwise putting yourself in a vulnerable position as you make the transition from being seated to being on your feet," he concluded.

He had them practice a few times and adjusted their positions. When the bell chimed, he went back to the front of the room and bowed. The students returned the bow. When they rose, he was gone and so was the temple. All the students were back in their clothes, standing in the middle of the lawn. The students from the other temples were heading back into the school. But the new students stood there, stunned and staring at the personalized handbook that had materialized in their hands. There was a bookmark on the first page, and it said *READ ME*.

CHAPTER 12

BRAIN FREEZE

WHEN LOLA GOT to the room to change before dinner, Sara was already there.

"A little heads-up about Master Smoke would have been nice!" she said as she flung her bag onto her bed. Sara was sitting at her desk making notes in her planner. She burst out laughing and turned around. "What? You didn't like the Temple?" she said innocently.

"What is he?" she asked.

"We're not exactly sure. He's some kind of Master of Illusion," said Sara.

"So that means none of what we saw was real? The Temples, the kimonos? But wait, we all had handbooks at the end—those were real," said Lola rubbing her temples. "And who was teaching in the other Temples?" she asked.

Sara laughed and replied, "It was him. He either clones himself or he can Astral Project himself to multiple places simultaneously. Again, not sure. I hope he'll tell us when we get to the University level. Those who have had the nerve to ask him never got responses. Only cryptic proverbs."

"And Lady Samsara, is she a High Elf Princess? How old is she?" asked Lola, brimming with questions.

"Again, we don't know and it would be rude to ask about her age," responded Sara.

Lola was shaking her head. "You've been here for five years and that's all you have?" she whined.

Sara was getting her towel and toiletries together to go shower. "Five summers, Lola! And in two weeks, there's not enough time to figure out all the mysteries of this place. Trust me. They discourage any kind of snooping. And I told you, they keep the younger kids busy. Don't worry, we'll get to the bottom of everything in the fall! Now come on, it's time to clean up if we don't want to be late for dinner," she said.

Lola wasn't ready, so she told her friend to go ahead. Once alone, she slipped into her robe out and stuffed her dirty clothes in the laundry bag so she could throw it in the chute as she went to the bathroom. Then she got her towel and toiletries and made for the showers.

EVERYONE WAS in high spirits at dinner. The Headmaster didn't have any announcements, so dinner began as soon as the Faculty were seated. The lavish fare was roast beef, butter and herb tossed carrots and green beans, with mashed potatoes. Lola was loving the food, and the dinner rolls were always slightly different at every meal. Tonight, they had star anise seeds in them. She couldn't wait to slather some butter on them. When the servers removed the cover of the dessert platter, Lola almost wept. Lemon squares—her favorite! After being told by her aunt and by Jackson that she was too skinny and could stand to gain a few pounds, Lola ate without abandon. Which always seemed to delight Devlin. He was asking the guys the same questions she had asked Sara about Master Smoke. Lola stopped eating to listen to their answer, but they had nothing new to add.

"Aren't you guys curious?" she asked no one in particular.

Colin replied, "We were when we got here at thirteen years old. But I guess we got used to there being a magical explanation for everything and stopped asking questions."

The others were nodding in agreement. Eating resumed and the conversation drifted to their plans for the remainder of the summer. James was saying he was having a house party for his birthday in August and he hoped they could all come. Lola was about to decline on account of the distance, but she remembered just in time that she could travel anywhere she wanted. For free and in no time at all! She sat back in her chair and sighed in contentment. Her eyes were closed, and she was smiling to herself in gratitude.

"You are not finished eating, are you? You barely ate," inquired Devlin with a worried expression.

She opened her eyes; the moment had passed. "No, I was just counting my blessings; a wonderful new family and home, good food, new friends, the ability to travel with my key. Life could be so much worse," she said dreamily.

Clara cocked her head and asked, "Have you been stealing herbs from Professor Elderberry's greenhouse?" Everybody chuckled at this.

Lenora was nodding gravely and said, "I think she may be Fey."

"I'm not crazy! I'm just grateful is all!" rebuked Lola defensively.

Colin put his hand on hers from across the table. "No love, you misunderstand. Fey doesn't mean crazy, it means fairy-like or whimsical. It's a compliment!" he explained gently.

Lola blushed and apologized. This was all very new to her and she really needed to brush up on her magical lore. She definitely needed to read all her textbooks. She'd always liked school, but this was the first time she was getting any kind of practical use out of her school subjects.

Clara told everyone she and her family were going to visit Iceland for two weeks as soon as the summer program was over. Lola asked if she had any siblings and Clara turned and pointed to a boy seated with the 13-year-olds. "That's Louis, he used to be adorable," she said. Then she pointed at twin boys at the 15-year-old's table. "Those heathens are Alexis and Alexandre," she stated. Then she sighed and added, "Then there is Jean, my older brother. He's nineteen years old and thinks he knows everything!"

"Wow!" said Lola. "That's a lot of boys! My heart goes out to you!" she added.

"What's wrong with boys?" asked Devlin, innocently.

"Nothing unless you have to share a single bathroom with them in a very tiny house!" replied Clara, her French accent getting thicker as she got more agitated. "I adore being here at school, living in the girls' dormitory where everyone is, mostly, tidy, pretty, and *agréable*." She said the last word in French and Lola thought it was lovely. "I can't wait for autumn so I can move in for the year!" she said.

Lola asked if they would have the same roommates in the fall. Sara asked if she was trying to dump her. Lola laughed and said, "Of course not!" Lenora explained that they would, unless one or both girls had a good reason to request a change. Then something occurred to Lola. She turned to Colin and James and asked if they were roommates.

"Aren't you the curious one!" said James with a wink.

"I'm sorry, but in the rules, it says boys can't go into the girls' dormitory and vice versa. I assume that's to discourage fraternization. But how do they account for fraternization between boys or between girls?" she asked, blushing again.

"I'm sure you've heard the expression *Curiosity Killed the Cat*. But I'll answer your question. Yes, we are roommates, but we will likely not be roommates in the fall, unfortunately," explained James.

"Unless we take a triple room," amended Colin.

"You see, in the fall registration kit, there is a rather personal questionnaire and sexual orientation is one of the questions. It's not as intrusive as you might think. The reasoning is quite sound. Teenagers are known for their mercurial emotions. The school wants to avoid pairing a couple as roommates because, should they break up, it would cause a lot of tension," explained James.

"If you are a homosexual and you ask to be matched with someone specific, then you have to agree to have a third person in your room to act as a buffer, or a chaperone as it were," James continued.

"Could I be your chaperone, then?" asked Devlin.

"Don't you like your roommate?" inquired Lola.

"I don't have one!" he replied. "I mean, there are two beds in my room. It's not a single room. It seems the person I was meant to share a room with never came or perhaps there was an odd number of boys this year," he added.

Both Colin and James replied, "Of course!" enthusiastically and at the same time.

Lola's brow was knitted again. She wasn't sure about this chaperone business or singling out gay people. Then again, it wouldn't be fair if gay people had more opportunities to fraternize than heterosexuals. This way made it difficult for everyone!

Clara saw Lola's expression and added, "It's not just for gay people. My twin brothers had to get a buffer as well, and it couldn't be our younger brother. Can you just imagine! They decided to split up and each get a roommate saying they spend enough time joined at the hip. I guess they don't want any twosome getting too much into their own bubble and not interacting with others."

"That makes total sense. I mean, we're here to learn. And I guess we're also meant to learn to live in a community," said Lola. She liked Clara's explanation and felt better about the whole situation. She smiled and passed her plate to James for seconds.

"And she's back," said Devlin, giving his own plate to Colin.

When dinner was over, they all went to the Common Room. They had coffee and Lola asked if anyone had summer jobs. They all laughed. She asked what was so funny and Lenora told her that they didn't need one. The school was free, and they didn't need money for gas or transit passes. Lola asked about pocket money to buy things or gifts. Clara said her parents gave her pocket money every week. All the others said their parents did the same, mostly in exchange for chores or watching their siblings.

"Doesn't your aunt give you pocket money?" asked Sara. Then whispered, "If you need money, do let me know. I can help."

Lola blushed and thanked her. She told her she had more than enough and was only being curious again. She was saved from having to give any further details when Devlin interrupted and suggested they head to the Library.

"Sure. Let me just run back to the room and get my books. Meet you at the Library in, say ten minutes?" said Lola.

Devlin checked his watch. It was eight-ten. "Perfect, see you then!" he said and left.

Lola said goodnight to everyone and told Sara she'd see her back at the room later.

As she was walking away, Colin whistled and James exclaimed, "Have fun on your study date." He emphasized the word *study* and made air quotes as he did. Everyone laughed.

Lola blushed and checked if the whole room had heard him. She mouthed *Stop it* soundlessly and fled the Common Room in total embarrassment.

CHAPTER 13
STUDY DATE

SURPRISINGLY, they were not alone in the library. They chose a table where they wouldn't disturb anyone and laid out their textbooks and notebooks. Lola took out her planner and looked at the assignments. She was getting anxious again. How were they going to get through all of this in an hour and a half? She closed her eyes and took a deep breath, trying to reach for a calmer, more focused state. She felt a hand rest on top of hers. She opened her eyes and looked at Devlin.

"Don't worry, we'll get through this," he said soothingly.

"There is just so much to do! I don't know where to start," Lola replied, panic rising again.

"What calls to you most? What are you burning to read? Go with your gut," he added, closing her planner.

Lola looked at the choices: *History of Magic*, *Magical Community*, *Latin*, *Herbology*, *Traveling*, and *Martial Arts*. She was really curious about the magical species so she pointed to that. Devlin grinned knowingly and nodded his agreement. Lola asked him the same question and he chose *Traveling*.

"Let's set a twenty-minute timer and read as much as we can and take notes," Devlin suggested.

"We don't have phones, how are we going to set a timer?" Lola asked.

"I have a sports watch, the old-school kind, not a smartwatch," he said as he showed her his wrist.

"It's electronic, does it work even here?" she quizzed.

Devlin nodded and set the timer. Then, as the countdown began, he showed it to Lola. They got cracking. They read in companionable silence, both very focused on the task and scribbling notes furiously. Lola hoped Devlin had good penmanship and that she would be able to easily read his notes.

She was pleased with her choice. The textbook was well written and engaging. She found out that the average lifespan of a Fairy was between 1000 to 1500 years. Dwarves lived roughly 195 years while the High Elves lived about 750 years. The most remarkable were the Goblins—they only lived to 60 years of age! That meant that Sir Kravchuk was probably pretty close to dying. Though the book did say they reached maturity at age eight, so he could easily be twenty-five years old for all she knew. She had taken copious notes on magical powers, physical attributes, diet, and things to watch out for. It felt like only a minute had gone by when the timer went off.

They both jumped a little and laughed. Devlin went first. He talked really fast, showing her his notes and pointing to passages of the book. There was so much more to Traveling than she had ever imagined. For instance, there were different incantations you could speak before Traveling that would enhance the experience. One of the most notable was rendering the door invisible on the other end so you could poke your head through and check that no one was about. *That would have been so useful during Phyllis' would-be kidnapping*, thought Lola.

Devlin's notes were neat, concise, and pertinent. She was so pleased that she told him so.

"What were you expecting?" he asked, looking only slightly affronted. "Don't answer. We don't have time," he added with a chuckle.

Lola shared her findings the same way he had. He too was fascinated by the information she had gathered and praised her notetaking and calligraphy. Lola asked how they would share notes and Devlin said they would figure that out later. He had her choose another topic. She chose *Herbology* and he chose *Martial Arts*. The countdown began.

The *Herbology* textbook was a work of art. All the pictures were hand drawn and the book itself seemed to have been written by hand in the most beautiful, flowery handwriting. It read like a storybook, giving the origins of the plants, both period and provenance. But it was also very well indexed and could easily be used as a reference book.

Each plant or flower had its own page. The top part of the page held the drawing. The middle outlined important facts in bullet form, and the bottom displayed a short anecdote. She found out that it was Basil Vinegar that Professor Elderberry had used to rouse her after her fainting episode. *Good to know*, thought Lola.

The timer went off and they had their mad-dash sharing. They were making really good time. Reading twenty minutes, then sharing five minutes each. When they were done, they each took one last topic. Lola took *Latin* and Devlin took *History of Magic*. And off they went.

Latin turned out to be even easier than Lola had thought. It really was very similar to Spanish, or rather the other way around. Languages based on Latin were called Roman, and the big five Roman languages are French, Spanish, Italian, Portuguese, and Romanian. She drafted easy-to-read charts in her notebook and was surprised again when the timer went off.

Devlin told her The Academy had been created over 300 years ago. It seemed that before then, magical beings learned from their families or apprenticed with an elder. There were no schools. But after the various witch hunts and witch trials all over the world, humans with magical abilities either stopped using them or went underground. Most magical non-human species either hid in remote areas on Earth or found refuge in other worlds or realms. To avoid losing the knowledge entirely, special schools were created and housed in worlds of their own for the students' safety.

Lola gave Devlin a quick rundown of her notes. They weren't

nearly as fascinating as Devlin's. The lights blinked; they were getting used to what that meant. Devlin checked his watch; it was nine-fifty and they had to be in their rooms by 10 p.m. As they gathered their textbooks, they tried to figure out how to share their notes. There was obviously not a copy machine in the library and it would take forever to copy them by hand. As they were discussing it, some other students passed them and one of them stopped.

"Sorry to interrupt, but I couldn't help overhearing. Are you trying to exchange notes?" he asked. It was the boy from the Martial Arts class. Devlin nodded.

"That's easy. You'll learn this in Latin 2. Give me two notebooks, one that has the notes and one to be copied to," he requested, gesturing with his hands. Lola and Devlin placed their notebooks on the table, side-by-side.

The boy placed his hands on each of the notebooks, closed his eyes and said, *"Notas Duplici Exemplari."* Identical notes appeared in the second notebook.

"Wow, that is so cool," exclaimed Lola.

Because they didn't have time to experiment for themselves, she whipped out one notebook after another and he spoke the incantation five more times.

"Thank you very much," said Devlin, looking ecstatic.

"How can we ever repay you?" asked Lola.

The boy smiled and took Lola's hand. She felt the urge to pull it free but remembered he was probably going to kiss it. Which he did as he said, "Perhaps you'll take a walk with me sometime when you're not so busy cramming."

He winked at her and left before she could reply. Lola was blushing, of course. When he was almost out of earshot she said, "Hey, what's your name?"

"Tom," he said.

"I'm Lola" she replied.

"I know," he answered and was gone.

Devlin was quickly packing up his notebooks, looking a little miffed. *Is he jealous?* She shoved everything in her satchel and they made a run for it. The librarian *tsked* at them as they went by and Lola shouted, "Sorry!" as she flew by.

They ran up the steps and whispered *Goodnight* to each other as they dashed into their respective dormitories. Lola ran down the hall, took out her key and rested against the door, panting, once she was safely inside.

"Ten p.m., on the dot. You are a brave girl," said Sara, looking up from her book just as the lights went out automatically.

Still panting, Lola made for her bed and figured she wouldn't die if she didn't brush her teeth before bed. Good thing she had showered before dinner. When she bumped her foot on the chest at the end of her bed, she heard a click, then saw a beam of light coming from the other side of the room. Sara lifted her flashlight over the bookcase to illuminate Lola's side of the room. "Thanks," whispered Lola as she got ready for bed. Once she was in, Sara switched the flashlight off and went back to her own bed.

Lola needed to relax a bit and clear her mind. It was still so full of knowledge and her heart was still racing. Whether that was from running or from Tom's attentions was unclear. Tom, though a year younger, was quite attractive and totally out of her league. He looked like he was the captain of the football team at his school and had most girls mooning over him. Nonetheless, Lola was flattered. Doubly so that it had made Devlin jealous.

She assumed going for a walk was the only date-like activity available to them here at The Academy. Despite her new friends' ribbing tonight, her time in the library with Devlin had not felt like a date at all. It felt like going to study with the perfect lab partner—efficient and expeditious. Despite his good looks, and spending a lot of time together, she really didn't know that much about Devlin. However, they had instantly settled into a comfortable companionship and she thought that was a good place to start any relationship, no matter where it led.

Lola's thoughts drifted to Jackson. They weren't officially dating, even though he had pretty much asked her to marry him . . . in the future. *This dating stuff is complicated.* Maybe she should just put it off for as long as possible. It seemed sensible to gather more information before she jumped in. Sara and the girls were bound to have good intel. Not only on dating in general, but on boys like Tom. Once that was settled in her mind, Lola drifted off into sleep.

CHAPTER 14
READY FOR ANYTHING

LOLA WOKE UP EARLY AGAIN. She did some yoga, poured a cup of coffee, and enjoyed her meditation. After a few failed attempts, she finally mastered the tie and slipped on her blazer. Filling her satchels with the morning's necessities, Lola scribbled a note for Sara and left their room.

She went down to the Common Room to see if there was any more coffee available as she figured it might be a quiet place to go over Devlin's notes before breakfast. The room was locked, so she crossed the hall to the Dining Room. It was a few minutes after six-thirty and the place was deserted. She went to the buffet table to check if the coffee was ready and it was. She did a mini victory dance and poured herself a cup, which she brought over to the table. She took out the *History* notebook and started to read.

She had just finished reading the *Martial Arts* notes and was about to get a refill when she heard shuffling feet near the doorway. She looked up and saw a few students start to trickle in, talking softly. She got another coffee and read the *Traveling* notes. While it was still relatively quiet, she re-read the notes she had taken for *Herbology, Latin*, and *Magical Communities*. By then, it was past seven-thirty and most of her classmates had arrived at the table. She was so engrossed that no one wanted to disturb her.

"I did the same thing," said Devlin as she was putting away her last notebook. "Except I went to the Greenhouse," he added.

"I thought of that but since Professor Elderberry asked if we wanted to help out, I felt bad just showing up to ask for some peace and quiet," replied Lola.

"I explained how we both needed to cram five summers' worth of information into one and she was most sympathetic. She said we were more than welcome," he stated before tucking into his massive plate of eggs and bacon. Lola said, "Okay," and headed for the buffet. She met with Sara and Clara on the way back to the table.

"Aren't you the early bird!" teased Sara. "I woke up at 7 a.m. and she was already gone," she said to Clara.

"I wanted to review yesterday's notes. There was so much going on that my head was spinning. I was just so tired last night that I was afraid we'd forgotten something," replied Lola.

They got to the table and ate quickly; there were less than thirty minutes until the end of breakfast. *There shouldn't be too many surprises this morning*, thought Lola. They had the same four classes, and it should just be just the two of them again.

When she was done eating, Lola sat back in her chair and tuned out a bit, relaxing. The boys were talking about a video game they all liked and were making plans to play together over the summer. The girls were discussing one of yesterday's classes. Lola was just about to go into a short, food-induced nap when the chime rang. "Here we go," she said getting up to put her dishes in the bins.

They all went to the east wing together and split up as they got to their classrooms. Lola reminded herself to introduce herself to the other students at their table as they would likely be in her classes in the fall. So far, there had been casual nods and smiles, but no real conversations.

When she and Devlin got to Dr. McClary's room, he was already at the front of the room and had written notes on the board for them.

"Good morning, Lola!" he said cheerfully. "Good morning, Devlin!" he added.

"Good morning, sir," they answered in unison as they walked down the row and took their seats.

"How did you make out with your reading assignment. Any questions?" he asked.

They both answered in the negative, and so he began his monologue and his pacing.

Today he talked about Pythagoras, whom Lola had only heard of in Algebra class. Apparently, the ancient Greek philosopher had brought forth the idea of reincarnation, as well as quite a few astronomy, science, and mathematical discoveries. He was said to have second sight and the ability to command beasts. The hour flew by and as the bell chimed, the professor left them with yet more chapters to read in their textbook.

Devlin and Lola walked over to the *Latin* class next. In the hall, Devlin stopped Lola and asked her if she thought they should discuss the note duplication spell with Dr. Thompson.

"I was thinking that at breakfast. But then it occurred to me that it might not be something we're supposed to be doing. It sounds like spellcasting. Maybe we should ask our friends instead. What do you think?" she said.

"I think you're right. We don't know if Tom knew about it because he learned in class or from a book, or a friend. We could try the spell for ourselves tonight in the library. Do you want to meet up again?" he asked.

"Devlin, I think you and I are study buddies for the foreseeable future. I hope you don't get sick of spending all this time with me," said Lola with a chuckle.

Devlin grinned as though he'd just won the lottery. "I'll never get sick of spending time with you, Lola," he said sheepishly.

Lola blushed and pulled him along to the next class.

Dr. Thompson had also written notes on the blackboard. He didn't ask if they had any questions but he did ask with a wink if they'd had a nice evening. Lola and Devlin looked at each other quizzically, wondering if they should respond. But it was obviously a rhetorical question because he launched into the days' lesson on conjugation.

He was a good lecturer but it was still a little boring. He either didn't notice or mind the glazed look in Lola and Devlin's eyes. He just kept on talking about the importance of distinguishing between perfect, pluperfect, and imperfect tenses.

Lola's brain decided it could simultaneously listen, take notes, and call up last night's encounter with Tom. He was just so yummy-looking. His raven hair was parted on the side and the silky bob was tucked behind his ears but for a rogue strand that fell over his right eye. *I wonder what it would feel to run my fingers through it; all tousled and wild. Would it give him the appearance of a pirate?* As squeaky clean as he appeared, Lola just knew he had layers, some of them dark and thrilling.

Lola was pulled from her dreamscape when Dr. Thompson whipped out a pop quiz, five minutes before the end of class. He looked exceedingly pleased with himself. He gave them each a copy and said to do as much as we could before the chime. Lola dived into the question on the paper and started scribbling the answers as fast as she could. He'd made a chart similar to the one she'd done in her notebook last night, so it was fairly easy. There were a few trick questions on vocabulary he had referred to yesterday, but as they were multiple-choice questions, those were easy enough. When she finished, she quickly scanned her answers and flipped over her paper and pushed it toward the teacher. He raised an eyebrow in question.

"Sorry, Doctor. It's the way we did it at my old school in a timed quiz. I guess I was overzealous," she said, her heart racing.

In the time it took her to say all that, Devlin finished his quiz, looked over at her, and did the same. Dr. Thompson took their papers, assigned some chapters to read, and dismissed them at the chime.

Next up was *Magical Communities*. Lola braced herself for the sight of the Goblin. She and Devlin stopped short upon entering Sir Kravchuk's classroom; he hadn't dismissed the previous group. It was the 13-year-olds' group. There were about fifteen of them and they were copying a sentence off the blackboard.

Students must remain quiet in class until given permission to speak. x 50

"Ms. Evers, Mr. Johansson, I'll be with you in a moment. You may be seated in my office while you wait for these green ones to learn their lesson," he said, overseeing the time-honored punishment.

They tiptoed around the outer perimeter of the class so as not to call attention to themselves. When they got to the office, they hesitated. He saw them hovering by the door and added, "Go on, have a seat. There might even be tea and scones in there if you like." He shooed them in with his hands to a chorus of envious groans from the kids in class.

They went in and gingerly sat down on the settee. It was so plush that despite sitting at opposite ends, they were pushed together as they sank down into it. They giggled nervously.

"Tea?" Devlin asked in a posh British accent.

"No, thank you, sir," Lola replied demurely fluttering her eyelashes.

They sat in silence with their bags in their laps, waiting to be summoned back into class. There was a fire in the hearth, but the room didn't seem overly warm. Lola distracted herself by taking in the room. It was a little stuffy and cluttered. She wondered if Goblins had a reputation for being hoarders. *Or perhaps that was Dwarves*, she thought. Still, the room had a cozy feel to it. It certainly looked lived in. She imagined the teachers spent most of their free time in their offices.

"Come on back, they've gone," bellowed Sir Kravchuk from the classroom.

They both got up so quickly that they bumped into each other and had to awkwardly disentangle their bags when the buckle on Devlin's bag caught the leather tassel on Lola's.

They made quick work of it as Devlin said, "Coming, Sir Kravchuk."

Seated in their usual spots, pens at the ready, they waited for the teacher to take his seat on his desk, grab his pipe, and begin.

In this lesson, he told them the story of how Men, Goblins, Dwarfs,

Gnomes, Elves (the short kind), Ogres, Trolls, and Giants were all related. He produced a large poster with something of a family tree on it. The main tree had three branches. The first on the left split in two, Elves and Dwarves. The middle branch also split in two, Gnomes on one end and the other split between Men and Goblins. The third branch split twice, once for Giants, then split twice again for Trolls and Ogres. From this graph, it was easy to see that Goblins were the closest to Men on the tree. He went on to explain various attributes for all but the Giants, Ogres, and Trolls, which were not covered in this class. He suggested they might read up on them in the library, should they be so inclined.

Dr. Kravchuk was quite entertaining in his obvious bias against Gnomes and Elves. He had nothing but good things to say about Dwarves. On the topic of Men, he stated enough had already been said.

The bell chimed and he rattled off a few chapters for them to read before the next class. *As though that wasn't tomorrow*, thought Lola sardonically.

On their way to *Herbology* class, they chatted about garden gnomes and wondered if there were any in the Greenhouse. Their conversation stopped abruptly upon seeing Headmaster Lianon talking with Professor Elderberry. They started to retreat to wait politely outside the door, but they were told to come in.

"Hello, Ms. Evers and Mr. Johansson," said the Headmaster.

"Hello, sir," they both answered.

"How are you settling in?" he asked.

"Great," said Lola while Devlin replied, "Wonderfully, sir."

"Good, good," he said. Then with an apologetic look, he said, "I'm afraid I'm going to have to steal one of you for a little while."

Devlin and Lola looked at each other, both trying to figure out who was in trouble.

As though reading their minds, he chuckled. "You're not in trouble, either of you. I just need a little one on one with each of you, to get to know you better," he explained soothingly.

Visibly relaxing, they smiled and nodded as they waited to find out who was first.

"We'll postpone today's lesson and I'll give you each a private tour of the Greenhouse so you know where to find the plants in your text-book," suggested Professor Elderberry.

"Lovely idea," said the Headmaster. "Ladies first?" he asked, motioning for Lola to precede him out the door. She waved goodbye to Devlin and headed out.

CHAPTER 15
HEADMASTER

ONCE IN THE HALL, the Headmaster matched her pace, despite being much taller than her. Lola estimated he had to be at least 6'8". He didn't have to bend down when entering a room, and since most doors were seven feet high, that seemed about right.

His hands were clasped behind his back casually and he wore a serene look on his face, like all was right with the world. Either Lola really wasn't in trouble or he was a supremely good actor.

They went down the hall in the direction of the Library. Between the door to the Library and the one to the Common Room, there was a door Lola hadn't noticed before. The Headmaster opened it and motioned for Lola to go ahead. It opened onto a flight of stairs with another door at the top.

"Go ahead and open it," he said when she was at the top of the stairs.

She turned the door handle and entered the room. It was huge! It was basically the same size as the Common Room and probably situated exactly over it. On the far wall was one of the largest windows Lola had ever seen. It was completely round, set about a foot off the floor and stopping about a foot from the ceiling, which was easily twelve feet high. She imagined the tall principal could stand in front of it and feel like it was a normal-sized window. In front of it was a large desk that seemed to have been carved out of a giant sequoia tree. The top was smooth and polished but unvarnished. It was exquisite.

On the left was a massive fireplace with something like a bear rug on the floor and two well-worn leather armchairs with matching leather footstools. To the right was a partition that Lola figured led to the Headmaster's living quarters.

He led them to the armchairs and invited Lola to sit down and asked if she wanted some tea. She declined politely and sat with her hands neatly folded on her lap. Her feet, crossed primly at the ankles, were dangling because her feet didn't touch the ground. These were High Elf chairs, to be sure.

"I like to get to know the students. I usually have more than enough time to observe and grab a quick chat here and there. But you and Mr. Johansson share a peculiar predicament. Not only have you arrived here late in the day, so to speak, but you also share similar backgrounds in the sense that you both had absentee fathers and were left orphaned upon your mothers' deaths. The fact that these deaths happened within days of one another may be an unhappy coincidence, but I find it suspicious. Especially since you were also both kept in the dark as to your heritage for so long," he said then paused to let that sink in.

Lola's eyes grew wide at the implication and her throat constricted. Her eyes watered but she tamped down on the tears and took a deep breath.

"Please continue, sir," she said stoically.

"Was there anything unusual about your upbringing? Did your mother have any friends or acquaintances you might have found strange?" he asked.

Lola shook her head.

"What about at your aunt's house since you've been there. Has there been any unusual activity? Other than finding out you can travel with a magic key, that is," he said with a warm smile.

Lola looked up at him. He stared right into her eyes. She could almost hear him say 'Go on, you can tell me' in her head. She wondered if High Elves had telepathic abilities. When she actually heard the word 'Yes' in her mind, she jumped and grabbed the armrests.

"You can read my mind?" she asked in a strained voice.

"I can communicate with you telepathically. It's not quite the same. I can only hear the thoughts you give me access to, in response to a question for example," he said out loud.

"Right. That's weird," she replied with a pout.

"I apologize for being intrusive, I only wanted to see if you had the ability too," he said sheepishly.

"Wait, what?" Lola asked, confused.

"The fact that you were able to ask me a question means you have a predisposition," he replied.

"I didn't ask a question. I was only wondering. I was actually mulling over telling you about something," she said honestly.

"It really doesn't matter at the moment. What matters is your well-being and safety. I don't mean to alarm you, but we are looking into every angle of this situation. We already know you are a Time Walker. That, in itself, is rare," he stated.

"How do you know?" asked Lola.

"Your key; it's different to regular traveling keys. Yours is a skeleton key, it can open any door," he explained. "Now what was it you were hesitant to share?" he added.

"Well, something unusual did happen after I arrived at the Evers Mansion," she said.

She told him about her dad's time traveling and about the kidnapping, the incantations, and the council meeting. She also talked about the lawyers, the ancestors, and what she remembered about the link to the Freemasons. He listened attentively and did not interrupt. He also asked a few clarifying questions when she was done. He seemed surprised to hear the Archives were in Old English since all the copies he had seen were in Latin.

"Lola, I believe I should have a chat with your aunt Phyllis and, perhaps, with your attorneys," he said.

When Lola's eyes grew wide again, he reassured her that no one was in trouble. He pondered aloud the reason that her father and her aunt had lived with the keys without ever attending The Academy and said that he needed to find out if it was the same for the families who had attended the council. He put forward that there might be a subset of Travelers The Academy didn't even know about since the first attorneys or perhaps the Freemasons had the Archives possibly translated into English for the settlers in America. Lola nodded, not sure if she was agreeing to something or just showing she understood what he was saying. *So many unanswered questions*, she thought.

"Yes, of course, you should talk to Phyllis. She has a friend on the council, Boris, the one who helped us during the kidnapping. He would probably know even more than her about it," said Lola, hoping she was being helpful.

"Thank you, Lola. I'm sure we'll get to the bottom of this and find out that everything is fine. But if it isn't, we want to be able to address any issues that may come up, and to do that we need all the available information," he said.

"Yes, sir," she said as she relaxed a little bit more.

"Now, if you don't mind fetching Mr. Johansson, I'll let you get back to Professor Elderberry for that tour," he said getting up and heading to open the door for her.

"Yes, of course. Thank you, sir," said Lola walking briskly to the door and down the steps.

She nearly ran down the hall and skidded to a stop in front of the door of the classroom. She smoothed down her uniform, checked her hair in the reflection of the frosted window, and took a deep breath to calm herself before opening the door. The classroom was empty so she headed to the Greenhouse. She couldn't see either of them so she called out, "Devlin? Professor Elderberry?"

"Down the left aisle!" said her teacher in a somewhat muffled voice.

"The Headmaster would like to see Devlin, now," she said, pitching her voice so she could be heard.

"On my way," said Devlin and she heard feet hurrying towards her. Soon he appeared at the end of the aisle. She gave him directions to the office and he told her where to find the *Herbology* teacher and they went their separate ways.

Lola went down the aisle calling for her professor since she couldn't see her. Eventually, she heard a buzzing sound off to her right. The pink *bee* was coming at her slowly, making patterns in the air to catch her attention. Lola laughed and said, "Yes, I can see you!" The bee flew ahead of her in the aisle and with a shimmer of the air turned back into Professor Elderberry.

"I didn't want to startle you this time," she said, shaking out her skirts, which were actually a pale lavender today. She even had lavender woven into her hair which was currently coiffed into a loose chignon.

"Are you ready for your tour?" she asked and Lola nodded that she was.

"Go and get your textbook and a pencil, you'll want to note the location of the plants as you go," she suggested.

Lola ran back to the classroom to get her things. Her teacher was waiting near the door and they began.

They started with the outer perimeter and then down the three center aisles. Almost all the plants in her textbook were here in the Greenhouse except for a handful which Professor Elderberry said were dangerous and strictly controlled. As they looped back to the model of the school, the teacher checked her watch.

"I'm afraid we won't have time to visit the outside grounds," she said, seeming a little disappointed.

"That's okay," said Lola. "We can go with Devlin next time," she added.

They went back to the classroom and the teacher gave her the reading assignment.

"You'll make sure Devlin gets it?" she asked.

"Yes, we do our reading and studying at the library every night, and I'll see him at dinner anyhow," Lola said.

"Lovely, I'll see you in class tomorrow—unless you want to come in the morning. It's really a beautiful place to watch the sunrise. There's a bench just outside the Greenhouse," she said, beaming.

"That sounds wonderful. I may just take you up on that!" replied Lola.

The chime rang and she gathered her things and headed out of the classroom.

In the hall, she met up with the others and they made their way to the Dining Room together. Devlin was already at the table when they arrived. He gave Lola a knowing look and she gave a slight nod and mouthed the word *later*. He nodded too and started chatting with the guys as they all waited impatiently for the trays to arrive.

They were not disappointed. Today, they could choose between three types of grilled sandwiches, ham and cheese paninis, lobster rolls, or brie and apple quesadillas. There was also coleslaw and potato salad. For dessert, chocolate chip cookies, and tiny fruit hand pies.

It is definitely worth four hours of summer school to eat lunches such as these, thought Lola as everyone started passing plates and talking animatedly about the morning's round of lessons.

CHAPTER 16
FREE PERIOD

AFTER RETRIEVING HER GYM BAG, Lola headed towards the Main Hall with the others for the afternoon classes. As she arrived, Professor Thunderbolt was already waiting to lead his group to the west wing. To their delight, Devlin and Lola got to join their friends for *Magic* class. The *Magic* classroom was similar to the one for *Traveling*; it had a proper classroom on one side and a practice room on the other side of the glass partition. The teacher asked Lola and Devlin to sit with more experienced students and to take notes. They would only be auditing in the next few classes. He gave them each a textbook to read—*The Rules of Magic, A Handbook for Non-Magical Beings.*

Lola sat with Sara and soon understood why they would only be observing. Until either of them mastered rudimentary Latin, it was pointless trying to read, let alone speak, any spells.

Professor Thunderbolt had a very large book on his desk that looked a lot like the Archives Lola had received and brought along in her chest. She figured teachers would request that she produce it when it was required, though none had done so. She leaned into Sara and asked her about the book.

"That's the Archives. A rare and valuable book of spells dating back to the beginning of Travelers. It was said to have been gifted to humans, with the keys, by the Ancestors, though I don't know who they are or where they came from," whispered Sara as the teacher was demonstrating the proper way to enunciate a specific spell for going ten seconds back in time.

Lola let that sink in. So it was a good thing she had left her copy of the Archives in her chest. She wondered if she should tell the Headmaster she had it with her. It was hard not to feel like she was in some kind of trouble. At the very least, someone in her family tree must have done something wrong down the line for them to be so different from all the other Travelers. Well, there was Devlin too. And probably those other Travelers on the council, but there was no way to tell. Maybe they had all attended the Academy. But why have a council with only a dozen or so families from all over the world? There was a dozen or so kids in each group of the summer program at the Academy. That meant there had to be at least fifty families of Travelers. Was this the only school? she wondered.

She needed to drop this and pay attention. Professor Thunderbolt ran through a handful of spells and then asked the students to go practice in pairs in the other room. When Lola and Devlin made to follow them, he kept them back, keeping an eye on the other students.

"There are only two afternoon classes at a time, so you won't be getting any private classes the way you do in the morning. I hear Lady Samsara saw you privately yesterday, but that's only because she has an intern this summer. As I do not have that privilege, you will need to catch up. You may use this time to study independently in the Library or you may audit the class like today. Either way, I'll be giving you reading assignments and checking on your progress," he said as he left to join the rest of the class.

"What do you think?" asked Lola.

"I think we should use this time to cram in the Library. What about you?" replied Devlin.

"I agree. Even though this is every shade of cool," said Lola, looking at Sara through the glass partition. She had just made herself invisible for a few seconds.

Devlin knocked on the partition to get the teacher's attention and pointed to the door, indicating that they were going to the Library. The teacher came to the door and told them to read the first five chapters and write down any questions they may have. They were to report back to class on Thursday to check-in and get their next assignment. They agreed, got their things, and made for the Library. They had a good forty minutes before the next class.

As they walked, Lola asked Devlin about his visit with the Headmaster.

"That was a very unusual visit!" he said.

"Well, go on, tell me. I'm dying here!" said Lola.

He looked around him to see if anyone might overhear and kept his voice low.

"Well, first off, did you notice he has a portal in his office?" he asked.

"A portal?" asked Lola, a confused look on her face.

"You know that huge round window in front of his desk, it's a portal," he said excitedly.

"A portal to where?" asked Lola, starting to think she may need to brush up on magical lore.

"Anywhere!" said Devlin, eyes huge, miming with his arms.

"How do you know?" asked Lola, her own eyes growing large.

"He told me, of course. Because I'm a World Jumper," he explained.

He was about to continue when they came across a few of the lunch servers rolling a cart of dirty dishes. They both smiled and only resumed talking when they got to the Library and, once there, only in hushed tones. They went to their usual table. They were the only ones there, and no one asked why they weren't in class. In fact, neither Lola nor Devlin even noticed if there was anyone at the counter, so intent were they on their discussion.

"He showed me what my marble is for," said Devlin, taking it out of his pocket.

Lola cocked her head and scowled at him, urging him to continue.

"It's a time and place marker. I place it in the control panel before I travel then carry it with me so I can come back to where I came from," he said in a very low voice, still checking to see if there was anyone about.

"Control panel? Like a fuse box???" questioned Lola, completely confused.

"No, it's kind of like a trackball computer mouse. There's a socket and you put the marble in it and the keypad lets you input your current location," he explained.

"What about your destination? If you can go to other worlds, is there a registry? A catalog to choose from? Or do you just flip through them like in that Doctor Strange movie?" she asked.

"Yes, it's kind of like the Doctor Strange movie thing. It's complicated. And I'll get private classes with the Headmaster in the fall. Just like you'll be getting private time travel classes, I'm sure," he said.

They sat there quietly for a while. Then Lola asked him what he thought of the spells the rest of their class were doing. They ended up talking the rest of the period and guiltily jumped when they heard the chime. They made their way to the Main Hall and Devlin told her how the Headmaster thought her mom's accident may not have been an accident at all and that they were looking into it. She told him the Headmaster was also looking into a bunch of stuff on her end and that he was going to summon her aunt for a chat.

They were soon joined by the rest of the gang who had already gotten dressed in preparation for the class. Lola raced up to their room, changed, and came back down just in time, if a little out of breath. Professor Brambles said she would surely enjoy the restful class. "You have no idea," said Lola under her breath, and Devlin, who had just arrived and was panting next to her, chuckled.

The *Mindfulness and Meditation* group followed the left path from the half-moon, where the Master had arranged his students into three lines. *These must be the advanced students; there aren't all that many of them.* Craning her neck, she spotted their friends in one of the lines and waved.

Their group followed the path around the building, then turned right at the next fork, towards the woods surrounding the dome. As they neared the end of the path, Lola saw there was a large wooden platform with benches all around. The students went to the benches and lifted up the seats. Arranged nearby were cushions they could take to sit in. Lola and Devlin grabbed a cushion and went to sit in an open spot. Lola recognized Tom—the boy who had helped duplicate their notes. He winked at her and she blushed and turned away quickly.

The teacher sat in the lotus position, facing them. She wore green silk harem pants and a loose flower print top. Her chestnut hair was split down the middle and hung loose down her back. She was serenity incarnate. *Just looking at her is soothing*, thought Lola. She had golden-colored skin and gold-flecked green eyes. She wore no make-up, but Lola thought she was easily the most beautiful woman she had ever seen. There was no telling how old she was. She was youthful without looking young and wise without looking old. An enigma, to be sure.

"Welcome back to *Mindfulness and Meditation*, it's a pleasure to see you all again. For our new students, I am Professor Brambles. Please follow along as best you can and I'll come to see you in a little while," she said, looking at Lola, then Devlin. They both nodded. Lola was a little self-conscious with everybody looking at her.

The teacher reached into her pocket and took out a miniature book. *Surely she can't read such a small book*, thought Lola naïvely. However, the book popped back into its normal size as she held it in her hand. Fairy magic! She went on to read a passage from the book while everyone listened attentively. When she was done, she asked for people's interpretation. A few hands went up, and she gave them each a turn to offer an opinion. She smiled at them serenely and shared with them they had great insight. With a wave of a hand, some light meditation music began. She had them close their eyes and breathe deeply. Her hypnotic voice led them on a guided meditation through the desert on a bright, sunny day, with a cornflower blue sky and the faintest warm breeze.

It was only when she heard the bell that Lola realized they had meditated for over thirty minutes. Well, some of them had. A few had fallen asleep and could be heard snoring. She heard some giggles and Professor Bramble's admonishment that sleep was the busy mind's way of getting the rest it requires. With a gentle hand, she went to rouse the slumbering students and resumed her position at the front of the class.

"Would anyone like to share their experience?" she asked.

Again, a few hands went up and students shared their experiences. Some of them seemed like out-of-body experiences, but Lola couldn't be sure. She was still new at this meditation business. With each exchange, Professor Brambles would exclaim how interesting or thought-provoking she found the experiences. With a bow and a *Namasté*, she dismissed the group but asked Lola and Devlin to stay behind for a quick chat.

"How did it go?" she asked them. "Was this your first experience with meditation?" she inquired.

Devlin looked at Lola and motioned her to go first.

"I've only just started. My aunt taught me. She said it would help to focus when traveling. But it also helps to deal with . . . everything," said Lola making large gestures with her hands.

Professor Brambles emitted a noise of understanding and turned to Devlin expectantly.

"Mother had a meditation practice and she taught me when I was young. We would meditate together a few times per week. I admit I have let it drop since she passed away, but today felt really good, so I think I'll get back into the habit," he said earnestly.

"Wonderful!" she said as she produced two mini textbooks from her pocket and handed them over. They stared at them, waiting for the pop, but nothing happened.

"Your assignment is to figure out how to get them back to regular size," she said and, spinning on herself, she disappeared.

Lola and Devlin just stood there as the wind of her retreat rustled their hair.

CHAPTER 17
TIRED

WHEN LOLA GOT into the room, she dropped everything and plopped onto her bed face first. Despite her thirty-minute meditation, she was bone tired. When she had pictured summer camp, she had imagined horseback riding, swimming in the lake, and singing around a campfire.

She heard the lock turn as Sara came into the room, who took one look at Lola and laughed. She then went over and joined Lola on the bed.

"Are you okay?" she asked.

"I just need a five-hundred-minute minute nap," replied Lola, her voice muffled by the pillow.

"Didn't you relax in M&M class?" asked Sara.

"I did; it was great. But my brain can't handle all this information in July," she replied.

Sara got up and dropped her own stuff. She gathered her toiletries and towel and headed for the shower. Before leaving she declared, "A shower will wash all the fatigue away."

Lola looked up and turned her head towards the door. "You think a shower cures everything," she said.

"No, silly, that's tea! However, would it perk you up to know I heard there's chocolate pie for dessert tonight?" she asked, trying to tempt her friend up from her bed.

Lola shot up and asked, "With whipped cream?"

"Is there any other way to serve it?" asked Sara. Lola was up in a flash and grabbing her towel and toiletry bag. Sara left with a smile on her face.

THERE WAS INDEED CHOCOLATE pie with whipped cream for dessert. There was also a twist on mac and cheese; fat, curly pasta drenched in a creamy, white cheddar sauce, served with buttery green and yellow string beans. Today's dinner rolls came with a tarragon butter that made Lola's eyes roll back in her head.

"Are you happy I got you off your bed?" asked Sara as Lola moaned over her dinner which everyone thought was hilarious. She wondered if they made the food this good so the kids wouldn't feel homesick.

"Yes. This is amazing," she said and gave her plate to Colin for mac and cheese seconds.

"I think I'll ask to move in here permanently," said Devlin, his mouth full of mac and cheese.

Lola laughed. *He gets it,* she thought. The rest of them took it for granted. Lola was more than aware that she was very fortunate to have been born in the Evers family and now be the heir to the family fortune. But she remembered weeks where there were just too many bills and her mom would make frank and beans for dinner, or the traditional mac and cheese that came from a box. Lola never complained; she thought everything tasted good.

Until Phyllis had cooked for her. And now every single meal at school felt like a five-star restaurant to her. And poor Devlin, all alone, having to cook for himself. No wonder he wanted to move in.

Lenora piped up and ask if they wanted to go play Hide and Seek in the woods after dinner. Colin and James were the first to say yes. Clara said she had other plans, to which eyebrows rose questioningly.

"Invite your plans to come along," said Lenora with a wink.

"It is too soon for that," said Clara cryptically.

Lenora's gaze fell on Lola and Devlin. "How about you lot?" she asked.

"Or do you have another big study date?" asked Sara elbowing Lola.

"It's not a date, we just have a lot to cram for and I don't want to have to spend the rest of my summer reading books for school like a nerd," replied Lola.

"I would love to go Hide and Seek. But Lola is right, we are so behind the rest of you, it isn't even funny and we have to take all the same classes in the fall," said Devlin.

"It's okay; we get that," said Sara. "We're just teasing," she added.

"I'm sure we'll be able to take a break over the weekend, right?" said Lola, turning to look at Devlin.

"Yeah, we'll be so sick of reading, and of each other, by then we'll beg you to play Hide and Seek!" he replied.

Everyone laughed and stuffed their faces with the chocolate pies.

AFTER DINNER, the gang headed for the Common Room to see if they could gather interest from their fellow classmates to play Hide and Seek. It was so much better when there were more of them. While the boys did a lap around the room, the girls discussed Lola and Devlin's relationship. The two had gone, yet again, to study at the Library.

The boys came back with a bunch of people, one of which was Clara's date. He asked if she was okay with him joining the group and, of course, she had to agree. The cat was out of the bag now; might as well go with it.

They proceeded towards the wood, passing some of the younger students playing 'Pass the Orb' with Sir Kravchuk.

"The rules are simple," explained Colin. "Everyone pairs up. One representative of each team will draw a straw, shortest counts first. The team counts aloud to one hundred while everyone else hides. Teams hide together; if one is spotted, both are out. Found teams must come back to the counting tree. All spells are allowed. If after fifteen minutes, the counting team has not found everyone, the game ends and a new counting team begins. Any questions?" he concluded.

Colin and James drew the short straw and began counting as the others scattered. When they started searching, James used an incantation for a light orb. They walked down the path, keeping an ear out for rustling leaves. The whole class had been practicing the invisibility and the sound bubble spell that day so tonight's game would be tight.

They took their time. Hide and Seek was fun, but there was an added incentive for the older students. Pairing up was not only for safety's sake, it also provided a little one-on-one time for couples.

There was a giggle to the left. James extinguished his orb and rendered himself soundless as he walked towards the sound. He had catlike reflexes and saw very well in the dark. He crouched low in the leaves and waited. None of the spells lasted very long. He heard the whisper and stretched out his hand and grabbed an arm. The owner let out a blood-curdling scream.

Colin rushed over with an orb. "Don't scream like that. The teachers will hear!" he chastised.

It was Amanda. She was a skittish girl, but she should have known better. This wasn't the first time she had played.

"Sorry, but you scared the life out of me!" she said, slapping James across the chest. "How can you be so sneaky?" she said getting up from behind the boulder she'd been crouching behind with her boyfriend Mark. The latter chuckled and led her back towards the counting tree while whispering in her ear. Soon, she could be heard giggling down the path.

When the fifteen-minute timer went off, Colin and James had found four of the five teams. Sara and Jacob were crowned champions and a new game began.

CHAPTER 18
LIBRARY

IN THE LIBRARY, Lola and Devlin continued the same way they had so far. Reading for twenty minutes, then sharing five minutes each. They each tried the duplication spell once and it actually worked! As they read the *Magic* handbook, they realized most of the spells in there were for protecting Travelers on their journeys, or for innocuous things like closing doors, or duplicating notes. Though they were curious, they didn't try any of the spells. They did, however, look for a spell to increase the size of their *Mindfulness and Meditation* book, but found none. Deciding they had another day to figure it out, they read ahead in the *Martial Arts* and *Traveling* Handbooks so they would have more time tomorrow. They also agreed to ask their friends about it. Maybe they would help.

As they were leaving the Library to head back to their dorms, they noticed the Headmaster was coming towards them. He held a finger up to halt them, so they waited for him to catch up.

"All caught up on today's reading?" he asked pleasantly.

"Yes sir," they both replied.

"Good, good. Mr. Johansson, if you don't mind going ahead. I'd like a word with Ms. Evers."

"Of course. Goodnight, sir. Goodnight, Lola," he said and left quickly.

They watched him go and the Headmaster turned to Lola.

"I wrote to your aunt this afternoon. She'll be coming in tomorrow, but I'm afraid you'll be in class," he said.

"That's fine, thank you for letting me know," said Lola politely.

"In her response to me, she mentioned you had come to school with the Archives," he said. He waited to see if she was going to respond. When she only stared at him, he continued. "Do you have the book in your room, Lola?" he asked.

"Yes, sir. It's in my chest. I was waiting for the teachers to ask me to bring it to class. It's quite heavy."

"But none of them did," he prompted.

"No, they didn't," she whispered.

"Do you know why?" he asked.

"I do now. I saw a similar one in the Magic class and asked Sara about it. She said it was rare. Which means none of the other students have their own copy, I presume," she ventured.

"You presume correctly. Have you shown it to anyone? Or told anyone about it?" he asked anxiously, his eyes piercing into hers as though probing her mind.

"No, sir," she stammered.

"I think it best if you bring it to me so I can keep it safe," he suggested.

"Now, sir?" Lola asked.

"I know it's late and it's past curfew, but I don't think it's safe for you to leave the book where it is," he said and started walking towards the Main Hall. Lola followed. When they got to the stairs, he stopped and pointed up.

"Run up and get it—put it in your school bag so no one sees it," he urged in a low murmur.

She ran up the stairs, down the hall and unlocked her door. The hall was illuminated by a faint light so students could get to the bathroom at night without tripping. Sara was reading in bed with a headlamp, waiting up for her.

"Where have you been? It's past ten p.m. Do you know how much trouble you can get in for this? And if you're found with a boy, that's even worse!" she whispered.

"I was with the Headmaster and he needs me to give him a book I brought from home," she said, dropping her bag and heading for her chest.

"Now?" she asked incredulously.

"Yes, now. He's waiting at the bottom of the stairs as we speak. I gotta hurry."

She opened her chest and fumbled for her own flashlight. She grabbed a spare pillowcase to put the book in. Then she opened the box where she had left the Archives, but it was empty. She opened the other box—it was empty too. She searched the rest of the chest, but the Archives was nowhere to be seen.

She went to the wall and tried to switch on the ceiling light, but it wouldn't turn on. She checked her bookcase in the hope she might have inadvertently placed it with her other books, but it wasn't there. Then she bit her lip and turned to Sara.

"Did you borrow a book from me?" she asked.

"No, why?" she said.

"It's not here and I swore I left it in my chest. No one comes in here except us two, right?" she asked.

"Right, though I imagine someone who works here has keys in case of emergency or if we lock ourselves out," said Sara.

"I better go see the Headmaster. He'll be wondering what's taking so long," Lola said and left the room to go tell him the bad news.

He didn't seem surprised. "I was afraid of this," he said.

"Maybe it went home, or to the attorneys. It kind of has a mind of its own," suggested Lola, hoping the book hadn't been stolen. She was the custodian of the Archives. This was bad. She started wringing her hands. The Headmaster put a hand on hers and told her not to worry. He would ask her aunt the next day and he was sure it would turn up sooner or later.

"Get some sleep. I've kept you up long enough," he said and

motioned for her to go up the stairs as he himself went back down the hall towards his rooms.

When she got back to the room, she told Sara she had been mistaken and that her aunt would send the book to the Headmaster. They said goodnight and she got into bed, once again, without brushing her teeth or washing her face. She tried not to obsess about the book or about the fact that Devlin and her mom's death may have been under unusual circumstances. She told herself to listen to her breathing. In and out. In and out. After a while, she fell asleep.

CHAPTER 19

FLYING

ONE WOULD THINK that going to bed late would help Lola wake up later, but she was up at the crack of dawn anyway. She had her routine down to a science. But today, instead of going to review her notes in the Dining Room as she had the previous day, she went to the Greenhouse for a much-needed hit of nature.

When she arrived, she called out to Professor Elderberry but got no response. She went down the main aisle and looked at the model trying to spot movement. She went around and thought she saw the Headmaster standing in front of his tall round window. When she squinted to see better, she swore he waved at her. Stupidly, she waved back and stepped away from the model.

She went to the outer doors and opened one of them. Before closing it again, she checked that it wasn't locked. She didn't want to be stranded and late for breakfast! The handle turned in her hand and she closed the door.

She looked around for the bench her teacher had mentioned, saw it in the distance and reached it with a few short strides. She would just sit and enjoy the stillness for a while. She slowed her breathing but kept her eyes open to appreciate the lush beauty of the grounds. She inhaled deeply and could smell the morning dew on the grass. She could feel the faintest breeze in her hair, and as the sun rose, it warmed her skin. It was bliss.

She tried to listen for birds or other sounds in the quiet, but she heard none. *Did they forget to create birds?* Despite the fact that she knew this was a fabricated world, Lola still enjoyed it. As she thought about it, she wondered what proof she had that her own world was real and this one was fake. Her musings were interrupted by the pink bee. However, it wasn't alone, as there was a blue bee with it. *It must be Professor Brambles.* The bees made a show of looping in front of her.

"Yes, I can see you, I won't be startled!" she yelled so the bees would understand. But no sooner had she said it, than she regretted it. She *was* startled when the blue bee turned out to be none other than Devlin! Professor Elderberry morphed elegantly and landed on her toes in mid-stride. Devlin fell to the ground in a heap with a thump.

"Devlin?" Lola said bewildered.

"Good morning, Lola! Isn't it a glorious day?" he said, panting, as he got up and brushed off his uniform.

Lola realized she was being rude and rose to greet her teacher.

"Good morning, Professor. You were right, it is beautiful out here," said Lola still trying to wrap her mind around seeing Devlin as a bee.

"Good morning, Lola. I had a feeling you'd enjoy it. Would you like to come and tour the grounds with me?" the Professor asked.

"As a bee?" Lola squeaked.

Professor Elderberry laughed. "As a miniature you with wings would be more accurate. But you can pretend to be a bee if you like," she replied.

"You have to try it, Lola, it's amazing. You get to FLY!" Devlin said as an endorsement. Then to their teacher he said, "If she goes, can I go again?"

Lola bit her lip and checked her watch.

"We'll be gone for no more than ten minutes. More than enough time to catch your breath and go to breakfast," said the teacher.

"Will there be any side effects?" Lola asked with a pained expression.

"You saw Devlin land, that's about the extent of injury you can expect. Just stick close to me and you'll be fine," she said reassuringly.

"Okay, then," was Lola's uncertain reply.

The professor got some sort of dust out of her pocket and blew it on Devlin and he immediately disappeared in a cloud, only to reappear as a blue bee. She turned to Lola and paused to ascertain if Lola was still willing. Lola nodded and in a whirl of golden dust, she was suspended in the air. There was a queer feeling in her stomach, like she'd done too many crunches. It was gone in a flash and as she opened her eyes, she had shrunk. Unable to catch a glimpse of her wings, she moved closer to Devlin to see his. They looked like bee wings.

Wait. Did I just fly over to Devlin by instinct? She was grinning like an idiot, as was Devlin. How did she know it was Devlin? she wondered, but the answer wouldn't come. The teacher appeared next to them and made a sound that Lola interpreted as *Follow me.*

They meandered off near the woods, close to the meditation platform. Professor Brambles was there, meditating. She didn't turn around when they passed. Once inside the woods, Lola was surprised to see there was ample light filtering through the trees, which seemed miles apart . . . to a bee. The teacher led them to a small lake bordered by wildflowers Lola couldn't name but recognized from her textbook. They set down on a huge flower, which looked like a sunflower but was bright pink. The sun was shining on the flower and they basked in its warmth for a little while before setting off again.

There was a path on the ground and they followed it. To them, it looked more like a highway. It led back out of the woods towards the door to the Main Hall. As they got nearer, they turned right and flew close to the school and peered into windows on the way. Everything was huge and was going by so fast it was hard to make any sense of it. After a while, Lola stopped trying to make sense of anything and focused on the joy of actually flying.

She felt so free and light as they rose high in the sky, looped, and then dove down at breakneck speeds. Lola should have been afraid of falling or crashing, but all she felt was exhilarated. She flew through a bush, and the leaves whipped past but never touched her as she weaved left and right, up and down.

With a sinking heart, she spotted the bench up ahead and knew it was almost over. In the blink of an eye, Professor Elderberry, then Devlin and then her, were back on solid ground. No wonder Devlin had crashed to the floor. She felt so heavy, like gravity was punishing her for her moments of buoyancy. Devlin reached a hand out to her and pulled her up. She brushed off her uniform and checked the state of her hair, the loose bun was still holding.

"What did you think?" asked Devlin eagerly.

"That was the most amazing thing I've ever done!" said Lola her face still shining with the rush.

"I'm glad you enjoyed it. It's a perk for those who come to help out in the Greenhouse," she said with a wink.

"Thank you very much, but I haven't helped in the Greenhouse yet," replied Lola, feeling a little guilty.

"The first one is free. The next one will cost you," said the teacher sassily and turned on her heels to go back into the Greenhouse.

Lola and Devlin followed behind her, mindful that it was time to go to breakfast. Lola thanked her Professor profusely and promised to come in the next morning to help out even if they didn't go flying. The Professor waved them off and told them she'd see them at fourth period.

On the way to the Dining Room, Lola asked Devlin if that was his first time.

"No. I came to see her yesterday and she took me to the outside vegetable garden. I actually cut the green beans we had for dinner yesterday!" he said excitedly.

"And here I thought the food appeared on the platters by magic. That means there are cooks and other staff lurking about. But all I've ever seen are the servers and the Faculty," mused Lola.

"The kitchens and laundry rooms are downstairs and there are secret staircases that connect all the floors," said Devlin matter-of-factly.

"How do you know all this?" asked Lola, fascinated.

"I asked the Headmaster on the first day," he replied.

"Aren't you the clever one? I was too busy fainting when I saw Sir Kravchuk. There was a nurse in the room, but I barely remember her. I think the room was under the stairs or something, but it's still a little blurry," said Lola as they went into the Dining Room.

They were the last to arrive. Lola immediately got a cup of coffee and started telling everyone about flying as a bee in the woods. They all stared at her, dumbfounded.

"You've all done that before, right? Like, when you were kids?" she asked, tentatively.

"No! I would definitely remember flying!" said Sara. They all started talking at the same time and asking a bunch of questions. Lola was very pleased to have the scoop on them, but demurred and let Devlin field the questions since it was his discovery.

"Professor Elderberry is new and only teaches the younger students. We should go introduce ourselves as she will be our *Herbology for Healing* teacher next year," suggested Lenora.

"We should go help out too," said James, looking at Colin who replied, "But that would require getting up early!" The look of horror on his face was priceless.

Lola laughed along with everyone and then she got up to get some food. Today, she was trying the chilaquiles—corn tortillas covered in green or red salsa with scrambled eggs with crumbled bacon on top. She topped them with cheese and sour cream and added a side of beans like she saw some of the other students do.

She got back to the table and dug straight in. She was not disappointed. Another moment of heaven for her taste buds. She went back for churros and chocolate sauce, which she thought was Mexican like the chilaquiles, but was told were actually a Spanish delicacy.

They were great dipped in coffee, too! She was still reveling in her third churro, rolled in cinnamon and sugar this time, when the lights blinked and it was time for class. She stuffed the rest of the churro in her mouth, licked her fingers, and downed her coffee, completely unaware that everyone was staring at her.

"What? Is it all over my face?" she asked, brushing invisible sugar from her around her mouth.

"You're like a five-year-old at the dessert table," said Colin, shaking his head with a rueful smile.

When he saw the look of dismay on Lola's face, James jumped in and said, "It's adorable to watch you eat." And with that, he put his arm around her and they walked to the east wing for first period.

CHAPTER 20
HAND CRAMPS

THE MORNING'S classes flew by. Lola wondered if there was a spell to keep her hands from cramping when taking so many notes. Better yet, she thought the notes should write themselves with a magic quill like that reporter in Harry Potter. But she had to admit the classes were fascinating. And with everything going on, she was very motivated to learn about the origins of magic, how to read Latin, and which magical abilities each of the species had.

By the time they got to *Herbology* class, Lola was looking forward to seeing Professor Elderberry for a proper class as they'd been interrupted a few times this week, and they must surely be behind.

She led them down the Greenhouse aisles, stopping at each plant and waiting for them to find it in their book and jot down the plant's location. The aisles were numbered and the plants were lettered. If there were more than twenty-six plants in an aisle, the following plants were lettered aa, bb, cc and so on.

She spoke briefly about each plant, not only reiterating the information they already had in their books, but expanding on it by sometimes adding an interesting use they would jot down right on the page.

"Professor, is there a plant or herb for muscle cramps?" Lola asked.

"There are many. Which muscles? What type of cramps?" asked the teacher.

"Hand cramps from taking too many notes in class," quipped Lola. Then she added quickly, "Other teachers' classes, not yours, of course."

Devlin laughed, as did Professor Elderberry.

"There are a number of options. Have you looked up *hand cramps* in the index at the back of the book?" she asked. But Devlin was way ahead of them and he recited, "Alfalfa, Chamomile, Valerian, and Wintergreen."

"Alfalfa you can eat, it has high levels of magnesium and that helps with cramps. Chamomile you can drink as a tea, it would also help you relax, or you can rub the oil into your hands. Valerian tincture is a mild sedative that will also relax tense muscles. As for Wintergreen oil, when mixed with a carrier oil, can be massaged into the skin. It contains methyl salicylate, which relieves pain and stimulates blood flow," she explained.

"Wow," said Lola, impressed. *This is really useful stuff!*

"You'll find Chamomile tea both in the Common Room and in the girl's kitchen. Before you go, I'll put a few drops of the oil in your hand and you can massage it in on your way to lunch," she said before resuming her lecture on the plants of the main aisle.

As promised, she put a few drops in Lola's hand and sent them off to lunch without an assignment, but requested they both come in the next morning to make up for the previous day's missed class. They both agreed and went to join their friends.

LUNCH WAS a blur of activity after Headmaster Lianon announced there would be a Social on Friday night. The noise level skyrocketed and Lola knew this announcement must have been important.

"What's a Social?" asked Devlin saving Lola from having to ask what must be a stupid question.

"It's a party. There's music, snacks, and people just hang out," said Lenora.

"It's usually outside and there's a bonfire with marshmallows and s'mores," added Clara.

"They even put up a dance floor and twinkle lights," said James wiggling his fingers in the air to illustrate the lights.

"It means no studying for you two. Mandatory attendance," put in Sara.

Lola and Devlin laughed.

"There is no way I would do homework on a Friday night, no matter how lame my social life is. Count me in!" replied Lola.

"What she said," added Devlin pointing at Lola with his thumb.

Finally the lunch trays were delivered and Lola couldn't resist clapping her hands excitedly as she saw stacks of grilled cheese sandwiches in endless variations: swiss, pepper jack, cheddar, gouda. Some with apple slices, some with bacon, others with roasted peppers and mushroom peeking out from inside. There was a large cauldron of tomato soup and a tray full of old-fashioned potato chips. As everyone filled their plates, Lola couldn't resist asking where the dessert tray was. This got chuckles out of everyone, but no one replied. She was starting to pout when Sara put her out of her misery.

"That means we're having ice cream. It'll come later. Don't worry," said Sara patting her friend's head like she would a child. Lola smiled and continued with her meal.

"What do we wear for the Social? I didn't bring much clothing, I assumed we'd be in uniform most of the time," asked Lola.

"Most people just wear something comfy, like jeans and a t-shirt, or lounge wear," said Colin.

"It's really not about the clothes you wear. It's about relaxing and getting to know other students outside of class," added James.

Lola smiled, but made a note to run through a few options with Sara at some point.

Just when Lola started feeling stuffed, the dessert trays arrived. It wasn't ice cream. It was better. It was homemade lemon sorbet with a piece of *Pizzelle* for garnish. It was sweet and tart and velvety. But there were no seconds. Lola sighed.

All too soon it was time to go back to class. She and Devlin headed directly to Lady Samsara's class, as she had suggested. They knocked on the door and tried the handle and found it was open. Taking her seat, Lola wondered what interesting trick they would learn today. Lady Samsara glided into the classroom and greeted them warmly. She asked if they had completed their reading assignment and they both nodded.

"Good. Today we'll practice focusing on precise locations and how to safely Travel with another."

They reviewed the handbook before moving to the other partition. She had them first Travel to coordinates on the floor. Then open a door for the other to pass through. When that was going well, she opened a door and had them follow her. They were in the Library!

Devlin was completely astonished. It was his first actual trip. They looked around to find a marker to focus on. The pair of armchairs in the corner would do nicely. Lady Samsara brought them back to the classroom and had them go to the armchairs in turn.

Once that was mastered, she had them pop into a few other places within the school and then outside on the grounds. They practiced peeking out to ensure no one was around. Suddenly, Devlin asked if they could go to his Dorm Room. Lady Samsara said she and Lola were not allowed in the boys' Dormitory.

"Also, students should not be in their Dorm Room during class unless they are ill," she added.

When they couldn't come up with any more places to visit, they went back to class. Since there was a little time left over, Lola decided to ask a few questions.

"Lady Samsara, should Traveling and any other magics we may be able to do be kept a secret from others?" asked Lola.

"That's a good question, Lola. It's okay to discuss it within your family, as they should all be Travelers, whether they have acquired any magical abilities or not. If you feel safe to do so, discussing it with extended family or close friends is also okay. However, it should never be made public, photographed, or recorded in any way. Not because it's a secret per se, but because we are not equipped to handle the inevitable fall out," cautioned Lady Samsara.

"Thanks. This is all new to me, to both of us really. The difference, for me, is that I Traveled before I arrived here, as did my aunt, but we didn't know about the handbook or the magic or anything else. So we're going to have a lot of catching up to do," said Lola.

"Feel free to ask if you have any other questions or concerns. Both of you," said Lady Samsara looking at Devlin.

When no more questions were forthcoming, she gave them their assignment and dismissed them. They went to change, then met up in the Main Hall and chatted while they waited for their *Martial Arts* class. As they were ready a few minutes before the chime, they were alone and so were the only ones to witness a door appear and Phyllis, of all people, step out.

"Aunt Phyllis!" cried Lola as she ran and hugged her tightly.

"Lola, what a welcome!" said Phyllis hugging her back. "Is this how you welcome all the visitors to the school?" she chided.

There was shuffling behind them and Lola saw it was Headmaster Lionan.

"Normally, we shake their hand warmly and ask if they'd like a spot of tea," he said taking her hand and drawing her away before the other students flocked to the Hall.

"I guess I'll see you on Sunday," said Lola with a sigh.

"Yes, darling. I can't wait!" said Phyllis, giving her a questioning look and discreetly pointing at Devlin. Lola mouthed *I'll tell you later* and waved goodbye.

"So that was your aunt?" said Devlin lamely.

"Yes. I'm sorry I didn't have time to introduce you," said Lola.

"That's all right. It all happened rather fast," he said.

Their conversation was drowned out as the chime rang and the students swarmed the Hall. Lola went to stand in line with the white belts and waved at her friends.

Today's class was grueling. After the short meditation, they practiced getting up a few times until everyone had mastered it. Then the Master demonstrated the five movements they would lean: Bear Crawl, Rolling forward over the shoulder, Rolling backwards over the shoulder, Hip escapes, and Break falls backwards.

They worked on those for most of the class. Lola was sweating and breathing hard. Eventually, the Master had them return to their spots around the room and sit cross-legged.

He explained that the point of this class was not to compete, fight, or even to rise to the next belt color. If Jiu-Jitsu was something they were passionate about and committed to mastering, he would teach them.

"The goal of this class is to get you into shape, make you aware, and give you tools to protect yourself if you find yourself in a tricky situation," he said.

He bowed and dismissed them.

CHAPTER 21
BOYS

IT HAD to be the best shower Lola had ever had. She knew she would be sore tomorrow, but the hot water cascading down her neck and shoulders would surely do her good. She'd have to check the *Herbology* book for what to take for muscle soreness. It was a good thing the next *Martial Arts* class wasn't until Friday. She'd definitely be doing some extra stretches before going to bed tonight.

When she got back to the room, Sara was already dressed and waiting for her. They hadn't had any real girl time since she was spending her evenings with Devlin at the Library. While she had her attention, she showed her the few outfits she had brought from home for downtime. She hadn't planned on wearing them outside their room, but Sara said those would do just fine for the Social.

"Also, do you know a guy named Tom? I think he's a year behind us," asked Lola as she hid on her side of the room and got dressed in her uniform for dinner.

"Tom? The very handsome but very naughty boy with long black hair and dreamy blue eyes? That Tom?" asked Sara, making her way over to Lola's side of the room.

Lola was done dressing, but she blushed at the look on Sara's face and the hands she had on her hips like Lola was hiding something.

"Why do you ask?" Sara said.

"Well, he was at the Library two nights ago and he showed us how to duplicate our notes. He keeps winking at me in class. I think he asked me out," said Lola, unsure.

"And you're only telling me this now?" screeched Sara. "And what do you mean you *think* he asked you out?" asked Sara.

"Well, he asked if I would go walking with him one evening when I wasn't so busy cramming," replied Lola.

"And what did you say?" she asked.

"Nothing really, I asked his name and I blushed," admitted Lola.

"And how did Devlin react?" quizzed Sara.

"He looked a little jealous, to be honest. But it's not like we're dating. We just have to spend a crazy amount of time together because of classes and studying," said Lola, adjusting her tie in front of the mirror.

"Do you like him? Devlin, I mean," asked Sara squeezing in to check herself in the mirror. It was almost time to go down to dinner.

"I guess. I mean he's very nice, we get along well. And he's gorgeous, don't get me wrong, but I'm not sure I like him *that way*," said Lola. "I really don't have much boy experience aside from Jackson," she added, feeling guilty now for some reason.

Sara asked if she was ready and they left the room to go down to dinner.

"Well, you probably haven't had much time to really talk if you're in class all day and reading all evening," said Sara as they walked down the hall.

"Exactly. I've barely had any time with *you* and we're roommates!" exclaimed Lola.

"Don't worry about that, we can catch up on Saturday. Meanwhile, about Tom. He acts like he's the great ladies' man, but Lenora is friends with his older sister. She's not here this summer, but you'll meet her in the fall when she comes to University. Anyway, Lenora spends a lot of time at their house and, according to her, he's the sweetest guy. Which is why Lenora has no use for him. You don't have anything to worry about. Besides, what's the worst that can happen here on campus where we're watched all the time and fraternization is forbidden?" asked Sara, winking innocently.

As they neared the stairs, Sara checked to see if Tom or any of his friends were around.

"His birthday is in August so he's actually the same age as us and will be attending school here in the fall because he's up for Custodian duty. If things don't pan out in the next couple of weeks, you'll have plenty of time later. Also, he's bound to have a big party for his birthday and you just might get invited," said Sara hopefully.

They were nearing the door to the Dining Room and Lola didn't want to discuss this around Devlin so she said quickly, "Wow, thanks for the 4-1-1. I'll probably see him at the Social on Friday. Maybe he'll approach me again. Anyway, let's drop it so feathers aren't ruffled at the table."

"You got it," said Sara as they headed for their table and greeted the boys who were already seated. Lola made an effort to smile at the other kids at their table and made a note to talk to them at Friday's Social. Lenora and Clara came in just before the Faculty came in so there was no time to chat before the lights blinked.

There were no announcements so the trays arrived soon after. Colin made his best snooty waiter impersonation and described the meal to the table, but mostly for Lola.

"For our American Foodie, tonight the chef presents veal parmigiana, fettuccini al pomodoro, garlic bread sticks, and tiramisu. My lady, may I have the honor of serving you?" he asked, hand out to take her plate.

Lola laughed and give him her plate and said, "*Si, prego!*"

She would henceforth be known as Foodie. As usual, the food was delicious and she enjoyed every single bite. Colin and James were talking about playing a game that Lola didn't know, after dinner. They included Lola and Devlin, but both of them wanted to stick to their routine.

"I don't know the game, maybe you could show me over the weekend?" she said to James.

"Yeah, sure. Don't worry about it," he said.

"So, who's coming back to school in the fall?" asked Lola. "I'm a little confused about how it all works," she added.

"All of us," said James.

"But we're not all the same age," countered Lola, confusion written all over her face.

"Students start their first summer when they are thirteen years old *before* the Summer Program begins. Students usually continue to attend until they graduate high school. If they choose to go to a regular University, then they have to attend until they are eighteen years old. So basically, it's six summers. However, anyone over sixteen who inherits Custodianship, and accepts it, is expected to attend school full time at the Academy. They'll quickly finish whatever high school credits need to be completed and then begin University. Otherwise, students who elect to attend University here, or those who are expected to inherit Custodian duties at a later date, will start here after they've completed their secondary education or high school. Depending on countries and birthdays, that can be anytime between seventeen and nineteen," explained James.

"Wait, we can refuse Custodian duties?" asked Lola.

"If you have a willing sibling of appropriate age, it can be transferred," said James.

"What if you don't have any siblings?" asked Devlin.

"Well, that would mean that you would also have to give up your key and I don't know anyone who wants to do that!" said Colin.

"Right, but what are Custodian duties anyway?" asked Lola.

"We're not meant to know until we're there. There's a class you have to take," said Lenora.

"Who else besides me is up for Custodianship?" asked Lola.

James raised his hand. "That's it?" asked Lola. "What about you?" she asked Devlin.

"I really have no idea. This is the first time I've heard about it," he said worriedly. "But if I'm last of my line, it would make sense that I'm meant to be Custodian as well," he added.

"That's enough talk about adulthood and responsibilities," said

Clara. "Let's talk about the Social," she added with a big smile, obviously trying to lighten the mood.

They talked about the party and Lenora asked if anyone else wanted to volunteer on the committee with her and Clara. They were pushing for a Hawaiian theme and said it was going to be a lot of fun. They had also petitioned for an extended curfew of midnight, but it was still under review. As it was, it was still scheduled for eleven o'clock.

The lights dimmed and the students were allowed to leave the Dining Room. Colin and James went to the Common Room. The girls headed for the dormitory. Lenora and Clara were meeting with Sasha, one of the girls in their year, in the girls' sitting room to work on party plans.

Sara said she was going to the room to read and Lola went with her to get her satchel.

"Sara, I know you said you haven't dated any of the boys here at school, but what about back home?" Lola asked while she was getting her things ready on her side of the room.

Sara had changed out of her school uniform and was brushing out her hair in front of the mirror. She looked at Lola through the glass and shook her head no.

"Nothing serious. I had a crush or two, but mostly we go out in groups. Why do you ask?"

Lola slung her satchel over her shoulder and came to stand next to Sara.

"I was hoping to ask for dating advice!" said Lola. "I've got to go, enjoy the peace and quiet!" she said on her way out the door.

"I'D LIKE to go up a little earlier tonight, if you don't mind," said Lola when she and Devlin were seated at their usual table in the Library. "For the past two nights, I got in past lights out and didn't brush my teeth and had to put my pajamas in the dark," she said laughing.

"Should be okay, we don't have a *Herbology* assignment and we've finished reading the *Martial Arts* Handbook," said Devlin.

"Right, but we need to figure out how to enlarge the mini textbook," said Lola.

"Let's look in the *Magic* textbook," suggested Devlin.

They were reading intently when a shadow appeared over Lola's shoulder. Speak of the raven-haired devil!

"What are you up to tonight?" asked Tom, aiming his megawatt smile at Lola. He was alone and Lola couldn't see if his friends were lurking about.

"We are trying to figure out how to read the *Mindfulness and Meditation* textbook," said Lola, showing him the miniature book in her hand.

He chuckled at that.

"Rookies! You're in the wrong book. You should have checked your *Latin* book," he said. He reached for the textbook, pressing very close to Lola, and placed it in front of her. Lola's face grew warm and she was willing it not to turn every shade of red. He leaned over, flipping through the book until he found the page he wanted. He placed a finger under the spell and encouraged Lola to try it. She sat back in her chair to look at Devlin. He was scowling but told her to try it. Tentatively, she said, "*Excresco.*" Nothing happened. Tom bent down so his face was at the same level as Lola's.

"No, it's *Excresco*. The letters 'sc' should sound like 'sh.'" The book popped like a kernel of corn, hovered briefly above the table and landed, full size, on the table.

"That's amazing!" said Lola clapping happily.

Devlin huffed, took out his own book and placed it on the table. He closed his eyes and took a deep breath and repeated the word, "*Excresco.*" His book did the same thing.

"Well done, mate," said Tom, clapping him on the back as he rose.

"All you have to do is speak Latin to do magic?" asked Lola.

He took out his key and waved it at them before dropping it back in his shirt.

"The key is where the magic happens. It's a conductor. Without it, nothing would happen," he said and started to move away from them. "I gotta go. It was nice seeing you again," he said, obviously talking to Lola.

"Thanks again for your help. I don't know what we would have done without you!" said Lola, immediately mortified that she was acting all flustered. And in front of Devlin, no less.

"You would have figured it out, I'm sure. Goodnight," he said and left them alone.

"Goodnight," she said to his back.

"Maybe we should head up as well. I'm a little tired," said Devlin, somewhat stiffly.

"But we haven't finished," said Lola. "We still have one topic to swap," she added.

"How about I give you my notebook for *Latin* and you duplicate your notes into it. Give me your *History* notebook and I'll duplicate my notes into it. Tomorrow when we have a free period, or should I say the *Magic* study period, we can review them together," he suggested.

"Okay, I guess that'll work. I should be able to concentrate a little while longer in the room," said Lola as she got up and gathered her things.

She wondered if she should say something. But Devlin hadn't said he liked her or asked her out. If she made out like he was jealous and he didn't actually have feelings for her, she would look like an idiot. It was possible that he was tired. Heck, she was tired. This way, she'd get to wash her face, brush her teeth, put on her jammies and finish up the *Latin* assignment well before lights out. She'd even have time for those stretches. And then she remembered the Chamomile tea Professor Elderberry had suggested. She'd get a cup and sip it as she read her *Latin* chapters.

CHAPTER 22

PROGRESS

LOLA AND DEVLIN met up at the doors of the dormitories at six-twenty the next morning. They hadn't planned on it, but it seemed they were somehow synchronized. They whispered, "Good Morning," to each other and set off for their early morning *Herbology* lesson.

On the way over, they exchanged notebooks and briefed one another on the previous night's reading. When they got to Professor Elderberry's classroom, she was waiting for them.

"Good morning, Lola, Devlin!" she said brightly. "Let's begin. Today we'll have a full proper lesson. No time for flying, I'm afraid," she continued.

"That's okay, Professor," said Lola, taking out her handbook and a pencil.

"Where did we leave off?" she asked.

"We finished the center aisle," replied Devlin.

She motioned for them to follow her and they went to the second aisle on the left. This one seemed to have plants with small berries. One by one, she told them about each plant, its care, and uses, and a few anecdotes.

"Professor," said Lola between plants, "this week we're basically covering *Herbology 1* and next week *Herbology 2*. Is that it?" she asked.

"Yes, dear," she answered.

"Will there be another textbook? Perhaps we could start reading it over the weekend," she suggested.

"Bless your heart, you *are* motivated!" she said with a laugh. "That won't be necessary. We like students to relax over the weekend. There is another textbook, more of a recipe book really. We'll work on tinctures and poultices next week," she continued.

When Lola didn't look convinced, she added, "We have plenty of time. With only two students—sharp, well-behaved, and disciplined students at that, we're really breezing through the material."

They got the two left aisles covered and then it was time for breakfast.

TODAY, Lola tried kedgeree: a dish made of basmati rice, smoked haddock, boiled eggs, peas, and curry. It was apparently a classic Scottish breakfast though, she would later be told, it actually came from India and was brought back by returning colonials in Victorian times. It looked good and she was feeling g brave, though she wasn't sure about having fish for breakfast.

When she got back to the table, no one said a thing. It must be more common in Europe than in America, she thought. She dug in and immediately congratulated herself on trying something new. It was absolutely delicious and filling. Though not so filling that she didn't go back for a few pastries to dunk in her coffee.

"So, how was your game night?" Lola asked Colin and James.

"It was great. We got a group of guys together and we were so into it that we almost broke curfew," said James enthusiastically.

The chime rang and they were off to their classes. The boys went off together, rehashing last night's game. The girls were talking about the Social, but Lola was in her own head.

She was happy to have semi-private classes since there was so much to cover, but she was looking forward to being part of the larger group. Which was surprising, as Lola had always been a loner. Hanging out mostly with Jane or reading in a corner by herself. For the most part, she had never felt like she fit in anywhere.

But it was different here. They all had something in common, and everyone was so accepting of others' differences. Granted, she was the only American in their group and they made fun of her insatiable appetite. But it was good-natured ribbing, the kind you did with good friends. She'd only met these people a few days ago, but they had already accepted her as one of their own. She smiled to herself then and Devlin offered a penny for her thoughts.

"What? Oh, hi. Isn't it wonderful to be here, and to have great new friends?" she exclaimed.

"Yes, you're right. I feel very fortunate to be part of this new family. Especially as I am now on my own," he said, nodding his head.

"I'm really sorry about that," said Lola, putting a hand on his arm gently.

"Thank you, but I have to admit this is the most interesting thing that has ever happened to me and I'm very glad to be here too," he said grinning.

Dr. McClary greeted them with a pop quiz. This one was not timed, thank goodness. Nonetheless, there was a healthy competition between Lola and Devlin and so they seemed to race one another to complete the test. While the teacher went over their tests, he had them take notes from the board. When she was done, Lola raised her hand to ask a question.

"Yes, Miss Evers," said the teacher.

"When are we going to learn about keys and marbles?" she asked.

"That is what the *History of Magical Artifacts* is for. We'll get to it once we've covered the contents of the previous course. By the look of your quiz, you are both being quite diligent with your reading so we'll get there soon enough," he said.

And with that, they moved on to the second textbook on the table —*History of Magical Worlds*. He had them turn to the center page which held a map. He moved to the side wall of the classroom and unfurled a similar, much larger and more detailed map.

"Some worlds are parallel to the human's world on Earth. The inhabitants live in the same space, only on a different plane of existence. To understand this fully, you need to understand what philosophers have been saying for millennia. There is only Here and Now. There is no time and there is no space. So everything we see in our world is ultimately an illusion. A construct, if you will, based on our beliefs and expectation. Which means that all of us, all species and beings, live here and now at the same time. Which is why it is possible to travel through time and space and how multiple worlds can occupy the same space," he said, looking to see if they were following before proceeding.

"This map was made for humans over a century ago in order to visualize the known worlds. But they are not actually in these physical locations," he said.

"You've probably heard of many of magical worlds you'll read about in this textbook. Perhaps not directly, but in stories, legends, and fairytales. Students usually enjoy finding out the truth about their favorite characters. Please read the first four chapters. I'll see you tomorrow," he concluded, just as the chime rang.

Dr. Thompson greeted them with a smile and exclaimed, "Welcome to *Advanced Latin*."

They took their seats and grabbed the second textbook on the table.

"The purpose of this class is for you to be able to read ancient texts which were written in Latin, or in other dead languages, which will be easier to decipher with a solid knowledge of Latin. You'll find most spellbooks are written in Latin. Let's look at the message I've written on the board. Can you figure it out? I'll give you fifteen minutes. You may work on it together," he said and went back to his office.

Phaedrus 1.24

Inops, potentem dum vult imitārī, perit.
in prātō quondam rāna conspexit bovem,
et tacta invidiā tantae magnitūdinis
rūgōsam inflāvit pellem. tum nātōs suōs
interrogāvit an bove esset lātior.
illī negārunt. rursus intendit cutem
maiōre nīsū, et similī quaesīvit modō,

quis maior esset. illī dixērunt "bovem".
novissimē indignāta, dum vult validius
inflāre sēsē, ruptō iacuit corpore.

Devlin got up and came to sit next to Lola. She started reading the second textbook which explained sentence structure while he used the first textbook to translate the words one by one.

"This would go a lot faster with Google Translate!" said Lola.

Devlin laughed and continued to work. Lola explained what she'd read, then offered to translate some of the remaining sentences. Fifteen minutes came and went, but the teacher didn't come back, so they kept going. After thirty minutes, they had come up with this:

A poor person, while wishing to imitate a powerful one, is ruined. In a meadow once a frog caught sight of a cow and, touched by envy at its great size, puffed up its wrinkled skin. Then it asked its children if it was bigger than the cow. They said "No". Again it stretched its skin with a greater effort, and asked in the same way, who was bigger. They said "The cow". Upset for the last time, while trying to puff itself up more mightily, it lay there with its body burst.

Lola slapped her forehead and exclaimed, "This is worse than Google Translate!"

Devlin laughed and said it was good enough to get the gist of it.

"Dr. Thompson?" he called out loudly. "We have completed the translation," he said.

The teacher popped his head out of his office and asked, "Well, what does it mean? In your own words."

Lola thought for a minute and replied, "Always be yourself?"

"Very good. Go through the first three chapters but only do the even-numbered exercises. You are dismissed," said the teacher as he went back to his office.

"That was actually fun," said Lola. "Is that a really dorky thing to admit?" she said.

"No, I enjoyed it too. I can't wait to read spell books and write spells, though I guess only Witches and Warlocks do that. It's still a little unclear what we can and cannot do," admitted Devlin.

The chime rang and they moved to Sir Kravchuk's classroom. There were ten drawings on the board, each numbered 1 to 10. It looked like there was a pop quiz here today as well.

The teacher gave them each a piece of parchment and asked them to identify the being, provide at least three distinguishing characteristics, three abilities, and three things to look out for. He went to his desk, grabbed a book and his pipe and said, "You may begin."

Devlin and Lola looked at each other and smiled. This was an easy test for them and they were going to race. It took them about twenty minutes, but Devlin handed his paper over first. Lola wanted to make one last pass to ensure she had not made any spelling errors. Sir Kravchuk gave their papers a cursory glance, found them acceptable and deemed them ready for Level 2—*Interacting with Magical Species.*

"You'll find the textbook on the table. This part of the class is all about etiquette. Just as you would learn about international customs before visiting a new country, you'll learn the customs of the beings living on Earth among the humans and those living on other worlds," he explained.

He waved his hand and everything but the Dwarf was erased. New notes appeared around the drawing.

"Though they may look jovial, Dwarves are very proud beings. They are quick to anger and can hold a grudge for a very long time," the teacher began. He continued his lecture on Dwarves for the rest of the class and gave them their reading assignment as the chime sounded.

In *Herbology* class, Professor Elderberry told them they would have a test the next day and they were welcome to come study and roam the Greenhouse in the morning if they wanted.

CHAPTER 23
USUS EST MAGISTER OPTIMUS

AFTER LUNCH, Lola and Devlin went to Professor Thunderbolt's class to pick up their assignment. In addition to their daily reading, he gave them a list of spells, in Latin, to identify and practice and sent them on their way.

As they made their way to the Library, they were both very animated and eager to start doing spells. As usual, the Library was empty. The Librarian, which Lola now knew was an elderly High Elf named Monara, looked up from her book and nodded to them as they passed.

They took the list of spells and started by translating them. It occurred to them, after the first one, that if they didn't get the pronunciation right, they wouldn't be able to do the spell. They tried each one out and made a star beside the ones that had failed so they could ask a teacher or one of their friends to help.

The first spell was for creating a window in a Traveling door so they could look out instead of poking their head through the door. That way the door remained invisible. *Smart*, thought Lola. When they tried it, it didn't work, but they wondered if it was because they were in the Library. They would try it in Lady Samsara's class the next day.

The next one was to create a small orb in your hand to light your way in the dark. "Handy," said Devlin as he tried it and marveled at the sheer blue sphere that appeared in his hand.

There was a fire-starter spell, but they decided to try that at the Social the next day, and most definitely outside.

"Look at this one, it's the one to turn yourself invisible for a few seconds," said Lola excitedly as she tried it. Nothing happened, so Devlin tried it with a slightly different pronunciation and it worked for him. Lola tried it again the way Devlin had and she disappeared! Lola was so excited that she whooped loudly then turned guiltily towards the Librarian and said she was sorry. They did it a few times so they could calculate how many seconds it worked for. The average was about fifteen.

"This one calls a drink of water," said Devlin, perplexed. That one stumped them, mostly because they were afraid of doing it in the Library and decided to try it on the way to the M&M class.

Another tricky one was the spell for shelter from the rain. It never rained here, so it was hard to test. Nonetheless, they tried it just to see what happened.

"Do you see anything?" asked Devlin who had just recited the words.

"There's a bit of a shimmer above your head. Hold on," said Lola. She tore out a page from her notebook and ripped it up into tiny pieces. Then she got up and tossed them over Devlin's head. The pieces cascaded around him but never touched him.

"Amazing!" cried Devlin. "You try!" he said as he picked up the papers from the floor.

Lola said the spell and Devlin tossed the papers. It worked! It was like she had an invisible umbrella above her head, which also extended like an aura a few inches around her body.

The last spell rendered them soundless. They tested that one by clapping their hands. On average, it lasted about thirty seconds.

"It would be useful if you have to hide in a closet or something," said Lola trying to think of other uses. "I wonder if it can render someone else quiet!" she said, eyes wide with mischief.

It didn't work but they figured there was a way to tweak it when their Latin was better.

They also decided that some of the spells would last longer with the addition of a word or two.

When the chime sounded, they packed up and headed for the Main Hall. Lola was looking forward to a relaxing hour with Professor Brambles.

As they walked towards the platform, Devlin, who had been walking ahead with some boys, ran back to her to remind her about the drink of water. He cupped a hand and said the spell. His hand filled with just enough water to drink without spilling over. Lola tried and exclaimed that the water tasted really good. Devlin smiled and walked quietly next to her the rest of the way.

Once they were seated on their mats, the professor read a Zen story.

There once lived an old farmer who had worked in his fields for many, many years. One day, his horse bolted away. His neighbors dropped in to commiserate with him. "What awful luck," they tut-tutted sympathetically, to which the farmer only replied, "We'll see."

Next morning, to everyone's surprise, the horse returned, bringing with it three other wild horses. "How amazing is that!" they exclaimed in excitement. The old man replied, "We'll see."

A day later, the farmer's son tried to mount one of the wild horses. He was thrown on the ground and broke his leg. Once more, the neighbors came by to express their sympathies for this stroke of bad luck. "We'll see," said the farmer politely.

The next day, the village had some visitors—military officers who had come with the purpose of drafting young men into the army. They passed over the farmer's son, thanks to his broken leg. The neighbors patted the farmer on his back—how lucky he was to not have his son join the army! "We'll see," was all that the farmer said!

"Let's sit with this and see what comes up," said the teacher and the meditation began. When the time was up, she sounded a bell. She led them through a few stretches and then asked what they thought the story meant.

"Nothing is ever good or bad. It just is," said a girl at the back that Lola couldn't see.

The teacher nodded and smiled. "Good, good. Anyone else?" she asked.

"Things are always working out for us, no matter how they initially appear," said the boy right next to Lola.

"Indeed," said the teacher and then she called on another student who had raised their hand.

"Don't jump to conclusions until you have all the facts," said a male voice Lola recognized. She dared to turn around and saw that it was Tom. He was looking right at her with a cryptic smile.

"Well done, Tom. As you can see, there are as many interpretations as there are individuals. Because everyone has their own unique experience," she added.

She put her hands out to the sides, and raised them up as she took in a deep breath. Then she lowered her hands and brought them together at heart center and said, "Namaste."

The students did the same and bowed. Then everyone started putting away the cushions.

Professor Brambles called to Lola and Devlin. "How are you getting along with the textbook," she inquired.

"Fine, it's very soothing to read," said Lola.

"Yes, I'm also enjoying it," replied Devlin.

"Wonderful, keep reading it and let me know if you have any questions," she said and then with a twirl of her finger she was gone.

They headed back silently. On their way, Devlin elbowed her and asked, "Are you thirsty?" A big cheesy grin was plastered on his face. They both called a drink of water and sighed happily as they walked back to school.

Lola headed straight for the shower, humming to herself and enjoying her blissed out state. In the hall, she passed Sara who said not to wait for her to go down to dinner as she was running late.

Lola had the room to herself to change and relax before dinner. Once dressed, she sat down on her bed and relished the first few minutes of leisure time she'd had in the last couple of days. She was daydreaming of how she could use the new magic spells she had learned to do. She couldn't wait to tell Phyllis and Jackson.

As she thought of Jackson, her eyes flew open. She would have to write a letter telling Phyllis whether or not it was okay for Jackson to visit on Sunday. Technically, he was like family, so there was no real reason why he couldn't come with Phyllis. However, from the Traveling Handbook, she knew Traveling with non-travelers was a tricky topic. They didn't say you couldn't, but they intimated that the permitted circumstances were for spouses and extended family. Jackson didn't actually qualify as either of those, yet.

The real question was whether or not she wanted him to come. She missed him, that was certain. But she also *didn't* miss him. It was a whole new world here at The Academy and she was realizing that everything she thought to be true in her old life may, in fact, not be true at all. Like the idea that they had to marry. That seemed more like a typical opulent southern family rule than a Traveling family rule. She needed more time to figure things out. To ask questions. To get some answers.

As if on cue, Sara came back from her shower. Lola checked the time and sat up. She shoved her dirty clothes in the laundry bag and decided to ask Sara for her opinion.

"Do you think Jackson should come visit with Aunt Phyllis on Sunday?" she asked.

Sara responded from the other side of the bookcase divider.

"Yes, of course he should come. Mostly so I can lay eyes on him and see if he's as handsome as you described him," she said.

"But he's neither family nor a spouse, so technically he shouldn't be allowed to tag along," replied Lola

"If he's not allowed, the door won't let him pass. It's as simple as that," said Sara walking to where Lola was waiting with her hand on the door. "Just let it ride and see what happens," she suggested.

"Sounds like a great way not to have to make a decision. I like it. Are you ready?" asked Lola.

Sara nodded and they left, walking briskly and dropping their laundry bags down the chute as they went.

CHAPTER 24

FRIENDSHIP

AT DINNER, once the Faculty had been seated, the lights blinked and the Headmaster headed for the podium.

"Dearest Faculty and Students. As you know, the Social Committee has been working very hard on tomorrow night's festivities. Here are a few logistics details. Participation is mandatory unless you are ill. That goes for the Faculty as well. If ill, you must remain in your room or quarters. Thus, everyone should be outside by eight-thirty. The dress code is casual. You are not required to wear your uniform, though you may do so if you wish. I am told the theme this week is Hawaiian. Drinks and snacks will be provided and outdoor restrooms will be made available. The festivities will end promptly at eleven. Lights out will be at eleven-thirty," he announced.

The students clapped and cheered at the extended curfew. The Headmaster raised a hand and the students were quiet again.

"On Saturday and Sunday, the breakfast buffet will be available from six-thirty to nine-thirty for those of you who may want to sleep in. Dinner will be served at the usual hour. In the afternoon, long chairs and parasols will be set up on the South Lawn for those wishing to bask in the sun. Collective sports will be organized on the East Lawn and those wanting silence and solitude may use the Meditation platform on the North Lawn.

"Lunch on Saturday will be an outdoor BBQ, available on the West Lawn from twelve-thirty to two-thirty. On Sunday, lunch will be picnic baskets to share with your visitors. Visiting hours are from one to four p.m. An outline of these events will be posted on the doors to your dormitories. Enjoy your evening meal," he concluded and headed for his seat where he nodded to the servers and the trays were promptly delivered.

"How do they know how many visitors we'll have to pack the picnic basket?" asked Lola.

"A letter is sent home on Saturday morning and your family will RSVP," explained Sara.

Lola nodded then, and without thinking, turned to Devlin.

"Devlin, would you like to eat with my family?"

Devlin looked relieved and immediately said, "Yes, I would love that. Thanks for suggesting it."

Lola was pleased. It would be awful not to have any visitors and having to eat alone.

Sara nudged Lola's thigh under the table and whispered, "What about Jackson?"

Lola made an *O* with her mouth and looked at her friend, with a panicked expression.

Sara patted her hand and whispered, "We'll talk later."

Lola didn't have time to obsess over it because a plate of food appeared in front of her. James had taken her plate and loaded it with what he thought she would like. Everything!

It was Moroccan night. There was chicken tagine with almonds, apricots, and olives, steamed couscous, and roasted beet and dandelion greens salad. She wasn't sure about eating dandelions greens, but they were okay, if somewhat bitter. For dessert, there was date cake with orange-blossom syrup and, of course, mint tea. It was all gloriously tasty and new. And the tea was really good, it was strong and sweet.

"You know that's actual tea, not herbal tea. There's loads of caffeine in it!" said Colin after she had poured her third cup.

Lola paused her cup midway to taking a sip, then shrugged and drank it.

"We've got lots of studying to do anyhow, right, Devlin?" she said as she elbowed him.

"Yeah, a lot," he replied and reached for the tea and poured himself an extra cup as well.

Conversation revolved around the Social and their weekend plans. Since most of their friends had multiple siblings, some here at school and others at home, they were relishing the Sunday visit and expecting chaos and mayhem. Lola told them she was only expecting her aunt Phyllis and perhaps Jackson, a close friend of the family.

At eight, the lights blinked and the students were allowed to leave the Dining Room. Most of them filed out and headed for the Common Room or for their Dorm Rooms.

Lola and Devlin bid their friends goodnight and left for the Library. They had agreed to bring their books down to dinner to avoid having to go back up to their rooms.

As they got to the Library, Devlin looked at Lola and seemed to want to say something but looked unsure.

"What is it? Do I have dandelion greens in my teeth?" she said picking at her teeth with a nail.

"No, that's not it," said Devlin, relaxing a little.

"Then what?" she asked.

"Is Jackson your aunt's boyfriend?" he inquired.

Lola burst out laughing and said, "No! Why do you ask?"

"Well, you said he was *a close family friend*. That's usually a euphemism for someone's boyfriend. Am I to understand then that he is *your* boyfriend?" he said, barely over a whisper.

"Oh. Well. Not exactly," floundered Lola. She had no idea how to explain Jackson to Devlin.

"Are you dating?" he asked.

Lola squirmed in her chair. She knew she should have discussed this with Sara first. She had been so focused on what to tell Jackson, she hadn't thought about Devlin's reaction at all. This might be proof that he had feelings about her after all. She needed to be straight, but gentle, with him.

"I mean, we only met recently. Jackson is nineteen but he's been working for the Evers family ever since his parents died in a fire. He handles the books and investments, but he's also our chauffeur and groundskeeper," she explained.

"You didn't answer the question," stated Devlin patiently.

"Right. Well, our families are very old-fashioned and they kind of betrothed us without our knowledge. It's archaic, I know. And we don't intend to just follow along blindly. But we've been spending time together and, though we do like each other, there's been no actual dating, yet."

"Has he kissed you?" inquired Devlin, stiffly.

Lola blushed. This was getting a little personal and awkward. But if Devlin was going to be a friend, she should treat him like a friend.

"Mostly on the cheek and forehead," she hedged, red-cheeked and embarrassed.

"Good! He's older and likely more experienced. A gentleman should never press his advantage on a young lady," he said, visibly relaxing.

Lola was glad she hadn't mentioned the two actual kisses they had shared. Or the fact that she had initiated the second one. Devlin was sure to think she was some kind of hussy.

"You sound like Phyllis!" guffawed Lola as she swatted him with her hand.

"Lola, you are a very pretty girl and you don't seem to be aware of the attention you are attracting from the boys around you. Am I right in assuming you have not yet started dating?" he asked.

Again, Lola blushed and hid her face behind her hands. "Why? Is it that obvious?" she asked.

"Not at all. It's just that unlike other girls your age, you seemed focused on your studies and not on flirting with boys. I assume you have not yet been bitten by the infatuation bug," he said. "Or perhaps you haven't met your true match," he ventured.

"What are you—Dr. Phil?" said Lola using humor to take the focus away from her love life. "If you've finished analyzing me, maybe we could get back to studying?" she suggested lightly.

"Yes, of course. I'm just trying to get all the facts. You are hard to figure out," he said as he opened the new History textbook. "I'll do *History*. Will you do *Latin*?" he asked hopefully.

Lola smiled and nodded, grabbing her *Latin* textbook and notebook. She was glad they had dropped the subject, but unclear as to where they stood. He still hadn't indicated he had feelings for her. She would wait and see.

They did their recap, duplicated their notes, and went on to *Magical Communities* and *Herbology*. Once that was taken care of, they agreed to read their *Mindfulness* manual on their own and to meet up at the Greenhouse in the morning to review for their test. They were done by nine-thirty and Lola was pleased.

As they walked back to the dorms, Devlin remarked joyfully, "Hey! We have the next three nights off!"

"Right, unless there's weekend homework. If there is, do you want to meet at the Library Saturday morning after breakfast?" Lola asked.

"Sure, no problem," he replied. Then he added, "Goodnight, Lola."

She waved at him from the Dorm door and went down the hall to her room. She was looking forward to a little downtime.

When she opened the door, Sara was reading in bed and mumbled a greeting, obviously taken with her book. *Perfect*, thought Lola. She got ready for bed, slid under the covers, and read the next chapter in her M&M textbook. It was a soothing thing to read right before bed and a great way to wrap up an interesting day.

CHAPTER 25
SCHOOL HOPPING

THE MORNING CLASSES WENT WELL, as did the *Herbology* Quiz. Lola had always liked school, but she was enjoying classes that she could put to use. She thought it was funny that she would get more use out of her *Magic, History*, and *Latin* classes than she would her *AP Maths, English Lit*, and *Science* classes.

Spirits were high at lunch. It was obvious that the weekend was fast approaching as the afternoon classes were considered by most students to be laidback. Lola didn't feel that way about *Martial Arts* class, though. That one was tough! Then again, it was probably more difficult for a nerdy bookworm like Lola than it was for the sporty types. It was a great way to push her limits.

In *Traveling* class, Lady Samsara had a surprise for them. They were going on a field trip!

"We're going to travel to a school for Witches and Wizards," she announced excitedly.

"Is it Hogwarts?" cried Devlin, eyes huge with excitement.

"That's a fictional school! No, we're going to the McTavish International Academy of Magical Sciences, in Scotland," she replied.

"Why are we going there?" asked Lola.

"It's a safe place to land, so to speak. My sister works there and she lets me take groups of students over. There may only be two of you, but when I take a whole group of twelve to fifteen students, it looks odd for us all to appear out of thin air," replied the teacher.

Lola and Devlin nodded. It made sense. No one at a magic school would bat an eye at strange people appearing, disappearing, or even doing magic.

"Do you have your keys?" she asked. They both fished them out from under their shirts.

"Should we get separated at some point, just take out your key, think The Academy, and you'll be back at the Main Hall in no time," she said.

They walked up to the Main Hall and Lady Samsara pulled open the Main Entrance door. But as Lola looked outside, it wasn't the usual layout of their school. There was a fountain up ahead. "Come along," said the teacher and they went outside. She closed the door behind her. They turned to face her and she said, "Welcome to Scotland!"

Behind her, they saw another set of double oak doors. There was an old-fashioned bell pull and Devlin asked if he could pull it. After a few moment's wait, the door was opened by a livered butler. Lady Samsara produced a calling card. He did not look at it but slipped it in his pocket.

"Lady Samsara to see Lady Mathilda," she announced regally.

The butler bowed slightly and motioned for them to enter. "I believe Lady Mathilda awaits you in her chamber, Lady Samsara. Do you require an escort?" he asked politely.

"No, thank you, sir. I know the way," she replied. He bowed again and closed the door.

"Come along, children," said their teacher walking purposefully past a large statue of Sir McTavish and down a dark and gloomy hall.

This school was not all sunny and inviting like The Academy. The walls looked like they were made of stone, like those of a very old castle. Lady Samsara motioned for them to follow her as she glided down the hall and stopped in front of a door and knocked. The door had a placard that read *Lady Mathilda*. The door swung open and both Lady Samsara and Lady Mathilda exclaimed, "Sister," in unison and jumped into each other's arms, hugging tightly. They were identical in every way except that Lady Mathilda was wearing an even more gorgeous and luminous silver gown than their teacher. It appeared that twins were a thing with the High Elves as well.

"Mathilda, here are the students I told you about. Lola, Devlin, this is my sister Lady Mathilda," said their teacher, beaming with pride as she introduced her sister.

Lola couldn't help herself. She curtsied, bowed her head, and squeaked out, "My Lady."

Taking his cue from Lola, Devlin bent at the waist with both hands clasped behind his back and said, "My Lady."

Lady Mathilda burst out laughing. "How precious you are, children!" Then looking at her sister she said, "Did you put them up to this, Samsara? Do come in!" and motioned for them to enter her rooms. The first room was her office and held a desk, a couple of armchairs, and a large cabinet. They followed her beyond it to a sunny sitting room where she invited them to sit down. She offered them tea, but they declined politely, having only just finished lunch.

"We don't have a lot of time. As you can see, these students are a little older than the ones I usually bring here," said their teacher. "Mathilda, do you fancy a little field trip?" she asked mischievously.

It was odd seeing Lady Samsara so excited and animated. She was usually calm and composed. She was absolutely giddy at this idea.

"What do you have in mind, Samsara?" replied her sister rubbing her hands in anticipation.

"We could have the children travel to a destination within your school, and each accompany one of them," suggested their teacher.

"How amusing! Yes, let's do that!" Lady Mathilda replied.

"How about you? Are you up for it?" she asked Devlin and Lola.

They shrugged and nodded. Surely they would be safe with two High Elf princesses inside a Magic school?

"Alright, I'll take Lola," said Samsara.

"And I'll take Devlin," countered Mathilda.

"Let's go back out into the hall," said Lady Mathilda and she took them back through the office and out the door.

"I'm going to describe a place to you. Close your eyes and try to imagine it. It's a large circular fountain made of carved sandstone. It spans about twenty feet across. There's an alabaster statue in the center. It's of a large apple tree. There's a young woman holding out an apple to someone. The water cascades up the tree and down from the branches into the pool below. The water is cool and clear," she described in a hypnotic voice. "Do you see it in your mind's eye?" she asked.

While she was describing it, both Lola and Devlin received a clear vision of it. It didn't come from their imagination. She had sent it to their minds. They looked at each other, bug-eyed, and said that they saw it.

"Good. Lola, take out your key and take us there," said Lady Samsara.

"Do the same, Devlin. We'll see you there!" replied Lady Mathilda.

They moved apart to have more room to maneuver. There was no one in the hall so Lola presumed it must be reserved for Faculty members.

Lola took out her key and closed her eyes. The image of the fountain was right there. She put the key in the lock and opened the door. She peeked her head out, saw it was safe to exit and went through it with Lady Samsara. They closed the door and waited for Devlin to arrive. It was but a moment and he and Lady Mathilda were there.

"Where to next?" asked their teacher.

As Lady Mathilda was going over her options. Lola asked, "Could we visit your Library?"

"Absolutely!" said Mathilda.

"Yes, however, do you know the incantation to make a window to look through your door?" asked Samsara.

"Yes, we learned it yesterday!" said Devlin.

"Perfect. Now pay attention. The Library is a long room. The center part has windows on either side and is only one story. That's where the work tables are. At the front of the Library is the Librarian's desk and small rooms that contain the restricted or valuable editions. At the back of the Library is the regular collection, on two levels, joined by a narrow wooden circular staircase. Do you see it?" she asked. They both nodded. "Off we go then!"

"Let's meet near the staircase. And don't forget the window so you don't hurt a library patron when opening your door," cautioned their teacher.

It went just as well the second time, and though both Devlin and Lola were enjoying themselves, the sisters really seemed to be having all the fun. It was obvious that Lady Matilda was thrilled at being included. They didn't cross paths with anyone at the Library.

"One more! Is there time?" asked Mathilda.

"Yes, a quick one," replied Samsara.

"Devlin, where would you like to go?" asked Mathilda.

"Is there a Music Room?" he asked.

"Yes! Though there might be a class in there, so the window will be important again," she said.

"But won't it disturb the lesson?" asked Lola.

"Yes! Won't that be hilarious!" exclaimed Mathilda gleefully. "The teacher, Mr. Spars, is so stuffy. It'll give the kids a good laugh. Besides, they need to get used to unprecedented events!" she cackled.

She closed her eyes and calmed down to describe the room to them. When she asked if they were ready, they both already had their keys out.

When she looked through the window, Lola could see there was indeed a class taking place. The students were playing together as an orchestra, conducted by their teacher, whose back was to Lola. Though there were no apparent obstacles, Lola was reticent to open the door and just walk into their classroom. Devlin, on the other hand, was as gleeful as Mathilda and they burst in and yelled, "Hello!" to the astonished group of children and their scowling teacher.

"Go on, dear, the damage is done," said her teacher, amused.

Lola opened the door and they crossed the threshold into the class. The students were applauding like this was the best magic trick they'd ever seen. Lola was mortified and she knew her face must be puce.

Devlin gave a bow and pretended to remove a top hat. Lady Mathilda curtsied. Lola waved lamely and Lady Samsara took a moment to go and see the music teacher to apologize. When she rejoined them, she announced, "Back to the Hall!"

Upon their return to the Hall, Lady Mathilda walked with them to the front door. She shook Lola and Devlin's hands. "It was a pleasure meeting you both," she said.

The sisters embraced and promised to see each other soon. Lola and Devlin thanked Lady Mathilda and followed their teacher through the door back to the Academy.

As they made their way back to the classroom to collect their items, Lady Samsara asked if they had enjoyed themselves.

"That was so much fun. Your sister is quite the mischief maker, isn't she?" said Devlin.

"Yes, she was always getting us into trouble. That's why I thought she'd enjoy the activity. She doesn't usually participate," she replied.

"Other than barging in on poor Mr. Spars, it was fun," said Lola, looking guilty.

"I'm glad you enjoyed it and I hope you enjoy the weekend!" she said as the chime sounded.

They thanked her and headed back towards the Main Hall for their *Martial Arts* class.

"What's your class like?" she asked Devlin as they headed outside.

"It's mostly sparring and learning new moves," he said.

"What belt color are you again?" she asked.

"Blue," he said. Then added, "See you later!" as he went to line up with his group.

The Master had them do push-ups, sit-ups, squats, lunges, chin-ups, with jumping jacks in between each. Then he reviewed the moves from Wednesday and had them partner up and practice. She was paired with a tall 14-year-old girl named Lana who was nice enough but not that chatty. Just when Lola's muscles were starting to shake, the Master called them back to the circle and led them through some stretches and then a short breathing meditation for winding down.

Walking back to school, she heard running footsteps behind her. Thinking it was Devlin or one of the gang, she stopped and turned around. It was Tom!

"Hey, Lola!" he said, panting beside her.

"Hey, Tom!" she replied and resumed walking.

"Will I see you at the Social?" he asked.

"Yes, it's mandatory," she replied deadpan.

He laughed and rushed ahead to open the door for her. As she walked past him, he said, "Save me a dance, will you?" and ran up the stairs to his dorm.

There was no time for a witty comeback, so Lola just said, "Sure," and watched him go in.

CHAPTER 26

SOCIAL

LOLA STARED WOEFULLY at the stairs and recoiled at the thought of climbing them. Her thighs were burning. *Where are the chamomile drops when you need them?* Then, on impulse, she turned and headed towards the Greenhouse hoping her teacher had a remedy for her. Professor Elderberry gave her a tiny cork-topped bottle to drink before bed and promised to teach her how to make some the following week.

She slipped it into her pocket and went back to the Main Hall where she decided to do a few more stretches before tackling the stairs.

"Lola, how was your class?" said Devlin as he strode in.

"Painful. Are you only just getting back from yours?" she asked.

"I stayed behind with the teacher. I had some questions," he said.

"Oh, okay," she replied.

"We should hit the showers so we're not late to dinner," he suggested.

"You go ahead, it might take me a while to get up there," replied Lola, grabbing onto the rail and using it to hoist herself up, one step at a time. Devlin asked if she was okay, and she waved him off. When he was at the top of the stairs, he turned and looked down at her. "Hey, Lola," he shouted. She looked up and waited expectantly.

"The guys told me there would be dancing tonight. Will you save me a dance?" he asked.

What is it with boys and asking a girl to dance in the Hall before the dance?

Again, at a loss for words, she replied, "Sure," and slowly made her way to her room.

"You're cutting it close," said Sara, already fully dressed and sitting at her desk, her hair still damp from her shower.

"I know!" Lola replied as she grabbed her stuff and hurried back out the door as fast as she was able.

Despite the late hour, she just couldn't rush the shower. It felt so good on her aching muscles. She stayed for as long as she dared and hoped the penalty for arriving late at dinner wasn't skipping dinner because she was starved.

Back in the room, Sara was gone so she dressed hurriedly. She just about ran down the empty hallway, pain etched on her face. She considered going down the stairs on her bum, but there just wasn't time for it so she gritted her teeth and flew down. She skidded to a stop in front of the Dining Room to catch her breath and compose herself. Students were chatting, so hopefully, the Faculty hadn't yet been seated. She went in and sagged with relief. Checking the clock above the door, it read five fifty-eight. She walked briskly to her table and poured herself into her seat with an exhale.

"I told you she would never miss a meal," said Colin, with a grin.

"Ha, ha," replied Lola, unamused.

When James was about to intervene, her face softened and she said, "I know, he was just teasing. And besides, he's right. I'm ravenous." They all laughed.

The Faculty came in. There were no announcements and the food was served post-haste.

In keeping with the Social's theme, they were having traditional Hawaiian fare. There was Kalua pork, chicken long rice, steamed manapua, and lomi lomi salmon. For dessert, hot malasadas—deep-fried balls of heaven coated in sugar. Lola liked it all. She wondered if the school served food from around the world so that students from all over the world would get a taste of home once in a while or if this was their way of preparing them for the culinary delights that awaited them on their Travels.

The Social was the hot topic. There was apparently going to be fancy dancing—the kind she had been terrible at in Williamsburg, but also the regular kind they could dance as a group. To her utter relief, both Colin and James also asked her to save a dance for them. Now she knew that it was a common thing to dance with friends. She didn't know why she had been worried. She had danced with a lot of boys back home at the social events she had attended with Phyllis. Then again, most of those were potential matches. It would make any girl antsy when a boy asked her to dance.

She was really looking forward to seeing Phyllis to ask about her meeting with the Headmaster. Also, she wondered when the Headmaster would call on them again to give them an update on his inquiries. Something was up, she could feel it.

"Earth to Lola!" said Sara.

"What?" said Lola jumping a little in her seat.

"You were miles away! We asked what you were planning on doing tomorrow afternoon," said James.

"Um . . ." Lola floundered.

"Remember, there's collective sports, tanning in the sun, and quiet time," said Colin reminding her of the options.

"I think I'd like to nap in the sun. I have a lot of books to read, but I'm just sick of reading right now. And I'll still be sore from *Martial Arts* class so I'm pretty sure I won't be signing up for sports," said Lola rolling her shoulders.

"Great! That's what we're doing too!" said Lenora.

"It's too bad there isn't a pool. We could have tanned in our bikinis," pouted Clara.

"I'm pretty sure that's WHY there isn't a pool. Besides, I don't do bikinis," replied Lola.

"Lola, how many boys have asked you to dance so far?" asked Lenora.

"Colin, James, Devlin, and Tom," she replied matter-of-factly.

"Tom?" shrieked Lenora.

"He's so handsome," said Clara dreamily.

"Yeah, he's been stalking her all week," put in Sara.

"He hasn't been stalking me!" denied Lola, huge eyes boring into Sara's. "And lower your voice, he might hear!" she added nervously.

"He has, actually," said Devlin who had been listening to the conversation. Lola turned to look at Tom's table, but he was deep in conversation with his friends. Devlin must have meant about the stalking.

"How would you know?" asked Lenora.

"We've been joined at the hip all week, remember?" replied Lola.

"He makes a point of coming to the Library when we're there," said Devlin.

"Well, well, well. He hasn't put that much effort into pursuing a girl in a while," said Lenora knowingly.

Lola, getting uncomfortable with the turn this conversation was taking, tried to change the subject.

"What kind of snacks will they be serving at the Social?" she asked innocently.

That had everyone in stitches. She never received a reply because the lights blinked and there was something close to a stampede as everyone went back to their rooms to change for the Social.

Lola put her dinner clothes on the back of her chair to wear again tomorrow. She'd only worn them for an hour, after all. She opened her chest and took out her jeans, a t-shirt, and her Chucks. She would feel much better with those than in yoga pants and a hoodie. She'd happily wear those in her room tomorrow morning after breakfast to lounge around. She was looking forward to sleeping in and a late breakfast. Probably more than this party, if she was honest.

"Are you ready?" Sara asked. "Or did you want to do something with your hair?"

Lola frowned and checked herself in the mirror. Her hair was loose and a little wild as she hadn't had time to do anything with it after the shower. She went to her toiletry bag and combed it out. Once she was done, she went to the door and asked, "Do I pass inspection now?"

Sara nodded and smiled ruefully. Her hair had been teased within an inch of its life. She was wearing makeup and hoop earrings. Lola wondered how she thought she was going to get away with those, but she said nothing.

They went down to the Hall and out the front door. It was a magical scene. The path to the Social was lit with hundreds of garden lights planted on either side. As they drew near the site, they saw a huge structure with a straw thatched-roof and four pillars to hold it up.

On one side was a refreshments table. There were drinks with umbrellas in pineapples and coconuts, grilled fruit kabobs, an assortment of finger food, and more malasadas! The rest of the space had to be the dance floor because the floor was a smooth wood platform. There was already Hawaiian music playing.

They were greeted by the Social Committee and had leis placed around their necks. The path continued towards the bonfire, already ablaze. There were tons of Adirondack chairs all around it with tables every few chairs that had s'mores kits and sticks for roasting marshmallows.

Lola decided she might forgo the dancing and just eat snacks. Not that she was hungry. She was still full from dinner. But the fire was so hypnotizing that she made a beeline towards the fire and sunk into one of the chairs. She sighed noisily and heard someone chuckle beside her. Of course, Tom would be sitting there.

"Oh, hi, sorry I didn't see you there. I just needed to chill," she babbled.

"No worries. You look tired. Want me to get you a drink?" he asked, getting up quickly.

"Um, sure. Thanks," she replied.

"Coconut or pineapple?" he asked.

"Surprise me!" she said.

He left and she went back to staring at the fire. He was gone for less than five minutes, returned with a coconut drink for her, and clinked it with his own.

"To your first Social!" he said.

"Thanks!" she replied with a smile.

He sat down in the chair next to hers and didn't say anything at first. Lola tasted the drink. It was good! Peach, orange, and coconut. She loved that there was also a little spear with maraschino cherries. Those were her favorite. She was aware that Tom was studying her and it was making her uncomfortable. Why was she so awkward around boys? To distract both of them she said, "So, Tom, tell me about yourself." Which she immediately regretted because it made her sound like one of those online dates.

He didn't seem put off by it and quickly responded, "What do you want to know?"

"Anything. Everything. You decide," she said berating herself for sounding way too eager.

Nonetheless, he made no barb or comment about it. He took a minute to gather his thoughts then turned to her and started talking.

"I'm fifteen, but it's my birthday soon so we're the same age. I have an older sister; you'll meet her in the fall. Her name is Tabitha and she's eighteen. You might have heard about her; she's friends with Lenora. I'll be finishing high school here in the fall because I'll be taking over Custodian duties ASAP since our dad died last April," he explained.

Lola had been listening and nodding. But at this she said, "I'm so sorry. Was he ill?"

"Yes, he had cancer and he'd been fighting it for a really long time. You can imagine that we were all relieved when he died. He's at peace now, but I'll miss him forever," he clarified.

"Wow, both my parents died of cancer. My mom died in May and my dad died when I was two," she said.

Tom's eyes grew large. "I'm so sorry, Lola!" he stammered.

"Maybe we can skip the sad bits and get to the fun bits?" she suggested, her eyes welling up and trying to tamp down the tears before they spilled. It was a party; she needed to get a hold of herself.

"Agreed!" he said quickly. "Want to roast marshmallows? That's fun, and tasty!" he said eagerly, shoving the bowl at her.

"That would be great!" she replied and smiled in spite of herself.

He got up to get some sticks. When he came back, he had put two marshmallows in his eye sockets and pretended to bump into her chair. She burst out laughing.

"Take those off before you land in the fire and we roast you for tomorrow's lunch," she chided, still giggling.

He seemed pleased to have made her laugh. He gave her a stick and she extended the bowl towards him. She took two for herself and slid them onto the stick, back-to-back.

"Evers, I like your style," he said, doing the same.

CHAPTER 27

DANCING

LOLA AND TOM had settled into a conversation about their respective families and general aspirations as they roasted and ate marshmallows. Tom was funny and soon Lola was relaxing. This wasn't so bad, she thought. We're just hanging out. Like with Jane. Or Jackson. Just because a boy was handsome didn't mean they couldn't hang out and be friends. It was absurd to be so nervous and tongue-tied around boys. You'd think she'd been in a convent all her life. She just had to learn to relax and be herself.

She heard the music change to classical pieces and tensed. Someone was bound to come to claim a dance. But they had to find her first. Tom was telling her about the trips he took every summer with his family. Last summer, they had gone to Egypt. He'd loved the desert landscapes and the Pyramids. Alexandria and Istanbul had been his favorite cities.

"I haven't really Traveled yet. I can't wait. My aunt goes just about every day, but I don't know where she goes. I know she likes Florence in Italy, and she has this Russian boyfriend who she only just found out was also a Traveler. It's a long story. I'll suggest we Travel together like you and your family. I'm sure she'd like that," said Lola. Tom nodded.

There was a lull in the conversation, with both of them staring at the fire. After a while, Tom looked at her and asked, "Lola, will you come to my birthday party? There will be a lot of people from school. In fact, most of your friends will be there."

"I'll have to ask my aunt. You live in Cork, right?" she asked.

"Yes. Is your aunt coming on Sunday? I could introduce myself so she has an idea of who I am when you ask her," he suggested.

"Um, yeah, sure. We can do that," said Lola.

He cocked his head and turned to the dancing hut. Grinning, he got up and held out his hand.

"I believe you owe me a dance," he said with a bow.

Lola groaned. "I'm a terrible dancer," she wailed.

"That is entirely beside the point. The man leads and I'm an excellent dancer. If I can't make us look good on the dance floor, I won't live up to my reputation," he exclaimed.

"Very well," she replied and put her hand in his. He pulled her up and tugged her onto the path.

The dance floor was already very crowded. Dancing seemed to be very popular. Even the Faculty was on the dance floor. Everybody but Lola could do it. Did they learn at school? Did their parents teach them? She was starting to fret and bite her lip.

"Lola!" said Tom sharply and her eyes snapped to his. "Stop whatever thought was going through your head. Dancing is fun. Come on, I've got you," he said reassuringly.

They took position on the outer perimeter. She placed one hand in his and the other on his shoulder. When she checked her feet, he raised her chin with a finger and *tsked* at her.

"Eyes up here," he said pointing at his eyes. "And breathe, Lola."

The music began and they started to move. Tom turned out to be a good dancer. He led her with a firm hand around her waist and a slight tug at her hand. The rhythm was getting faster and the momentum carried them off. It was some sort of jig. And there was spinning involved. Soon Lola was laughing with her head back like she was riding a merry-go-round. *Dancing* was *fun*, she thought.

When the music stopped, Lola was exhilarated and out of breath.

But she wanted to keep dancing. At Tom's questioning look, she grinned and nodded. They were all set for the next song when James came to claim her for a dance. Tom relinquished her and bowed to James.

James was a great dancer too, though a little more formal. He asked how things were going with Tom and she said they were going fine. Then, he made funny remarks on the other couples dancing and had Lola in stitches. Many of their teachers were dancing with one another, having a good time. When the song ended, she was doubled over trying to regain her composure.

When she got back up, Colin was there waiting for her. More bowing. She waved at James as Colin carried her away and blew him a kiss. He laughed. Colin was not amused.

"Are you trying to steal my boyfriend?" he asked, stone-faced.

Lola sobered and immediately said, "No! Absolutely not! I'm so sorry."

Colin laughed. "I'm just messing with you," he said and then he grabbed her waist and her hand and launched them into a fast-paced waltz. He led more loosely than her two previous dance partners and the steps were coming quicker. She was afraid she would stumble and go crashing down in the middle of the dance floor. Seeing her worry, he tightened his grip on her waist and winked at her. "You need a firm hand, filly," he said with a terrible western accent. Lola burst out laughing and relaxed for the rest of the dance. By the end, she was a little dizzy and hoping no one would claim her just yet.

Colin thanked her for the dance and moved on to his next partner, Sara. Lola moved away from the dance floor and came face to face with Devlin, who was holding two pineapple drinks.

"I thought you might be thirsty," he said handing her one.

"Oh, how thoughtful. Thank you," she replied, taking a sip from the drink. It tasted like Hawaiian Punch!

"Will you walk with me?" he asked, indicating the torch-lit path.

"Alright, lead the way!" she said and laughed at her own joke.

"What's so funny," he asked.

"Well, I've been dancing and boys keep saying they should lead . . ." she replied. It sounded lame now, even to her ears.

Devlin laughed lightly and took her free hand, which he threaded through his arm to rest on his forearm. It was a very formal way of walking. Or perhaps it was called strolling. And she felt like she should have been wearing a ballroom gown instead of jeans and Chucks.

"Hey, we don't have any assignments over the weekend. So, I'm going to stay in my room and relax," she said breaking the silence.

"Okay, great. I'm going to play a strategy game with the guys," he replied.

He was explaining the game as they looped back to the dance floor, but Lola wasn't paying much attention. She was still thinking about Tom. Devlin asked if she was done with her drink and then took both empty pineapples and placed them on the dumbwaiter. Then he turned to Lola, hand extended, and said, "How about that dance, now?"

She took his hand and he led her onto the floor. It was a slower dance and Devlin was a serious dancer, though very graceful. She remembered him telling her he had taken lessons as a boy. He was looking at her strangely.

"Is there something wrong?" she asked as he led her expertly around the room.

"I have a delicate question to ask you," he said with a pained expression.

This is it, she thought. "Go ahead, ask me anything," she said, feigning a relaxed attitude.

"It's about Sara," he began.

"Sara? What's wrong with Sara?" she asked, worried now that something had happened to her friend and looking around her to see if she was around. Her steps faltered, but he got her back on track.

"Nothing's wrong with Sara. Don't worry," he said soothingly.

"Well, spit it out then," she said, a little too sternly.

"Is she dating anyone?" he blurted out.

Lola relaxed and started laughing with relief. Not only was there nothing wrong with Sara, but Devlin didn't like *her*. He liked Sara!

"No, not at the moment. Why do you ask?" she asked innocently.

"I like her and would like to ask her out on a date," he said. "Do you think she likes me?" he asked.

"Everyone likes you, Devlin!" said Lola. It was the best she could come up with. She and Sara had only talked about Devlin regarding her, not Sara. Then again, if Sara thought Lola and Devlin might be a thing, she may not have been forthcoming with any feelings she might have about him.

"That's not what I'm asking," he said, pained.

"I know. The truth is, I don't know. She thought you liked *me*," explained Lola.

He made an *O* with his mouth and his brows furrowed.

"Is that what you thought, too?" he asked softly.

"Um, kinda," she said, her cheeks warming.

"Lola, I'm so sorry. I do like you, but in a good friend kind of way," he hurried to say.

"Don't worry! I feel the same way and I'm very relieved you don't have feelings for me! It was getting awkward," she said, resting her head lightly on his chest in relief.

They both laughed and Lola asked if he'd danced with Sara yet. Since he hadn't, she suggested he go for a stroll with her afterwards and just ask her out. The worst that could happen is she would say no.

"That's a splendid plan!" he said gratefully.

"But Devlin, why did you get all upset when Tom kept popping up?" she asked.

"I don't trust his intentions. He's got the look of a player about him and I don't think he's right for you," he said holding her a little closer, protectively.

"That's very sweet. But Lenora has vouched for him. And besides, we've only just danced and talked. He'll figure out what kind of girl I am soon enough," she said. He seemed mollified. "Remind me to give you my two cents about that Jackson fellow as well," he said.

Lola nodded and wondered ruefully if perhaps Devlin would be a better source of dating advice than any of the girls.

The dance came to an end and there was Tom to claim her again. She was happy to see him and she settled comfortably in his arms.

Contrary to Devlin, he wasn't so tall that she couldn't see his eyes as they danced. He had a great smile, and he smiled most of the time. He was charming and funny and Lola could feel herself falling for him more and more.

When the dance ended, the Headmaster announced it was the last formal dance of the evening. A more contemporary selection would begin after a fifteen-minute break.

Lola and Tom moved to the refreshments table. Now that they had worked up an appetite, Lola loaded her plate joyfully. Tom just smiled at her and tucked a strand of her hair behind her ear. Lola blushed and asked, "Aren't you eating? Or are you going to let me eat all by myself?" He chuckled, grabbed a plate and loaded twice as much food on it than Lola had. Finally, a fellow foodie!

The dance floor was crowded and it was getting rowdy by the fire, so Tom suggested they go sit on a bench along one of the unlit paths. It wasn't in complete darkness as it was illuminated by a lamp post not too far away. Lola agreed. They grabbed a drink and headed for the bench.

They ate and talked easily for a while. When the music started up again, Tom asked if Lola wanted to dance and she said no, but he could go ahead if he wanted to.

"I prefer to stay here and talk with you. Is that okay?" he asked.

"I'd like that," she replied.

It was only when the music stopped and the lights blinked that Lola realized the party was over and it was time to go in. They walked back to the dance floor to drop off their plates and empty drinks. Tom asked if he could walk her home and Lola was happy it was dark and he couldn't see the extent of her blush.

"Yes, thank you," she said demurely.

As they started down the path, he took her hand and they threaded their fingers together. They walked in silence and entered the Hall. It was empty. They went up the stairs and stopped in front of the girls' Dormitory.

"I had a great time tonight," said Tom, putting his other hand on top of their joined hands.

"Me too," replied Lola, grinning from ear to ear.

Tom took their hands and turned them so that Lola's was on top and kissed it.

"I hope we can spend more time getting to know one another. Soon," he said.

"I'd like that. A lot," replied Lola, beet red from the kiss on the hand.

He let go of her hand and pulled her in for a hug. She hugged him back tightly, holding on for just a little too long because his hug felt like it came straight out of the dryer—warm and electric!

He released her and she took a step back reluctantly, gaze on the floor. Facing him now would be awkward, she mused. But it wasn't. His midnight gaze locked with hers and he simply said, "Goodnight, Lola."

Spellbound, Lola replied, "Goodnight, Tom," and floated all the way to her room.

CHAPTER 28

WIZARDS AND WARLOCKS

LOLA GOT ready for bed while she waited for Sara to arrive. There was so much to talk about.

When she came in and saw Lola was already in bed, she and held up a finger and said, "Let me brush my teeth and grab my stuff before lights out. We need to talk."

She dashed to the bathroom, came back and jumped on Lola's bed.

"I barely saw you all night. Dish!" she said.

"Well, I ate roasted marshmallows with Tom. Then I danced with all the boys who had asked me. Twice with Tom. Then we had a private chat and snack on a bench. That's it," said Lola grinning.

"What do you mean, that's it. Did you kiss?" she asked.

"No!" cried Lola. "Well, he kissed my hand when he said goodnight, does that count?" she added.

"Absolutely not! Did you hold hands at least?" asked Sara.

"Yes! And he said he's looking forward to seeing more of me. Oh, and he asked if I could introduce him to Phyllis so she would know who he is and let me go to his birthday party," Lola said in rapid succession. "But the best part was the hug before we said goodnight. I can't describe how it felt, but it was amazing," she added dreamily.

"Good, very good!" said Sara nodding her head.

Just then, the lights blinked. Two minutes to lights out. Sara was getting up and heading to her bed.

"Wait, I have even more exciting news to share!" said Lola.

"What could possibly be more exciting than your evening with Tom?" asked Sara in disbelief.

"Guess who likes *you*?" asked Lola grinning like a fool.

"Who?" said Sara, just as the lights went out. She came back closer to Lola and they started whispering.

"Devlin! Didn't he talk to you when you danced?" asked Lola.

"I didn't get a chance to dance with him. I mean we all danced as a group when you were MIA. But no formal dance," she replied.

"Oh, that's too bad. Anyway, do you like him?" asked Lola.

"Um, well, I thought he like *you*," she hedged.

"I know! So did I! I'm so relieved. He thinks of me as a good friend. It's all good. Now will you answer the questions so we can get to sleep?" urged Lola.

"Yes! He's gorgeous and adorable. He looks like a cherub. And he's so considerate," sighed Sara as she headed for bed.

"Sweet dreams, Sara," said Lola, just above a whisper.

"You too, Lola," replied Sara.

LOLA WOKE at seven-thirty and stretched in bed like it was the greatest luxury. It felt good to sleep in. She cocked an ear, but there was no sound coming from Sara's side of the bed. She sat up, crossed her legs, and started her morning meditation. She did twenty minutes without being disturbed. Getting up, she left the room to go to the bathroom and grab a cup of coffee. When she came back, Sara was still asleep. She rolled out her yoga mat and did her usual routine while adding extra stretches for her thigh and calf muscles. The tonic Professor Elderberry had given her had worked wonders. She wasn't as sore as she thought she would be, but it never hurt to stretch a little more.

She got dressed and checked the time. If Sara wanted to eat, she needed to get up. But they hadn't discussed it. Maybe she planned to skip breakfast entirely. Lola was torn. *Better safe than sorry.*

"Sara," she whispered.

There was a moan.

"It's eight-thirty, are you coming to breakfast?" asked Lola, a little louder.

There was another moan and a shaking of the head. Lola guessed that meant no and left the room.

At their table, Lola was the only girl. Even the gang at the other end of the table had only male representatives. Just her and the guys.

"Good morning, gentleman. What luck to have you all to myself," she said as she sat down.

"We wondered when you'd come down. There was no way you were skipping a meal," said Colin jokingly.

"You're quite right," she replied, used to this by now. She had another jolt of caffeine and went to check out the buffet.

It appeared waffles and pancakes were a Saturday staple here as well. Lola was delighted. She placed a crispy Belgian waffle covered with sugar on her plate. Then she added a bunch of berries and topped them with whipped cream. She got a side of bacon, a few pieces of brie, some raspberry jam, and a croissant. Her mouth was watering. So intent was she on her plate that she nearly bumped into someone. Someone tall. She looked up into Tom's grinning face.

"I know you haven't eaten in a fortnight, but you really should watch where you're going," he teased.

"Sorry," she replied lamely, a goofy grin on her face. She couldn't stop smiling.

"You seem to have a few open spaces at your table; mind if I join you?" he asked.

"Yeah, sure. Is that allowed?" she asked, looking towards the Faculty table. Sir Kravchuk was eating alone.

"Let's be rebels!" he joked. He let her pass before him and he followed her to the table.

Colin elbowed James who was deep in conversation with Devlin.

"What?" snapped James. Colin was nodding in Lola's direction. "Oh, hello, Tom. Nice of you to join us," he said smoothly.

They sat down and started to eat. Colin started chatting with Tom about his upcoming birthday party. Asking about themes and costumes. Lola groaned. *Couldn't anyone have a party where people wore jeans, ate chips, and drank pop?*

She focused on her food and the delicious coffee she couldn't get enough of. She'd have to ask what kind it was so they could buy some for home.

The boys had finished eating and they got up, even the ones at the other end of the table.

"Fancy a game of W&W, Tom?" asked Colin, oblivious to James making eyes at him.

Tom looked up and replied, "Sure, but I'll join you a little later."

"We'll be in the Common Room," said Devlin as they left.

Once they were out of earshot, Lola asked what W&W was.

"Finally alone!" said Tom, wiggling his eyebrows and Lola laughed. "It's like Dungeons and Dragons, but it's called Wizards and Warlocks," he explained.

"I wonder why they didn't ask me to play?" she mused.

"It's not called *Witches* and Warlocks, now is it?" he said with a wink.

"That's sexist!" she said indignantly.

"It's a nerdy, boring game. You wouldn't like it," he replied to pacify her.

"But I *am* nerdy and boring!" she exclaimed.

"You may be nerdy, but you are most definitely not boring," he stated.

Lola had finished her waffle and bacon. She was dipping half her croissant in her coffee while slathering butter, jam, and brie on the other half, oblivious to the affectionate smile on Tom's face.

"Lola, what are you doing after breakfast?" asked Tom.

"I had planned on crawling back into bed and reading a novel until it's time to go outside for the BBQ," she said before stuffing the last bit of croissant in her mouth. She chewed a bit and then added, "You?"

"I had planned to go play nerdy, boring games with the boys," he said. "How about we go for a little stroll before we tackle those plans?" he suggested.

"Sure, it'll give me a chance to digest all this food. I might fall into a food-induced coma if I head straight to bed," she replied with a laugh.

"Are you finished?" he asked, trying not to smile.

"Yes, I'm stuffed. Let's go," she replied.

They got up and headed to the Main Hall and out the door.

"I keep expecting someone to ask where we're going," she said.

"The rules are clear and most students conform. They really don't need to be keeping an eye on us 24/7," he replied.

"But what about the younger kids?" she asked.

"Oh, they headed out on an adventure early this morning. They'll be back for lunch," he said cryptically.

"Do tell!" Lola exclaimed.

"A Traveling field trip, not sure where, but I remember going on them the past two years," he explained.

"Oh, we had one of those yesterday," she said, smiling at the memory.

"You and Devlin?" he asked.

"Yes. Lady Samsara took us to her sister's school and they each chaperoned us from spot to spot. It was fun," replied Lola.

"That's right, you only recently got your key. I know you haven't Traveled much, but have you ever used your key on your own?" he asked as they took the path leading to the back of the school. As their hands brushed, Tom latched on to Lola's hand. It felt wonderful to Lola. Like having a beautiful day, every day.

"Not much at all," she said. "I'm looking forward to doing just that when the summer program wraps up."

"I see. Coming to my party is going to be a big deal then?" he said, nodding with understanding.

"In more ways than you think!" she said.

"What do you mean?" he asked as they switched paths so they could loop to the front of the school.

"I know Traveling anywhere takes the same amount of time and energy, but Cork is a long way from Williamsburg, Virginia. Also, it's one of those formal parties with dancing and champagne. As lovely as those are, I'm never quite comfortable. I've only just had my coming out and I had zero preparation. Two months ago, I was living in a walk-up with my mom in Baltimore. Then, all of a sudden, I'm an heiress, I live in a Mansion, and I've got this magical key that lets me Travel anywhere I want."

Lola stopped talking and put her hand on her mouth. "I'm sorry, that was a bit of an overshare," she said turning bright red.

Tom stopped walking and turned to face Lola. "I'm happy you feel comfortable enough with me to tell me about your life, Lola," he said earnestly. "It means you trust me," he added.

Lola smiled a little, embarrassed. He pulled her in for a hug and rested his chin on her head. "You can always talk to me. If you have a problem or a question, I'll try my best to help."

Lola felt weak in the knees and she hung on to his arms. He smelled like she imagined a sports commercial would—strong and manly. He kissed the top of her head and stroked the hair at the back of her head.

"Shall we resume our stroll, milady?" he said, extending his arm. She took it and pretended to fan herself and fluttered her eyelashes, "Why yes, sir, do let's."

They walked back to the Main Hall where Tom kissed her cheek and said he'd see her at lunch. He headed for the Common Room and Lola went up to her room.

CHAPTER 29

BBQ

WHEN LOLA GOT BACK to the room, Sara was still asleep. She put her pajamas back on, grabbed her book, and plopped on the bed. Her bed was so comfy. She slid under the covers and tried to focus on her book. After all of five minutes, she gave up and fell asleep.

When she woke up, it was noon and she could hear Sara writing at her desk.

"Hey, Sara," she said, sitting up in her bed and rubbing her eyes.

"Hey! I'm writing to my mother to ask her to bring me some more books. Gimme a minute," she said for the other side of the bookcase partition.

Lola got up and stretched. She put on her gym clothes since that would be most comfortable for an outdoor picnic. When she was dressed, she went over to Sara's side and plopped on her bed.

Sara was folding the letter and sending it. Lola hadn't tried that trick since sending her sizing sheet back to school. It was really cool. Sara had her gym clothes on too, Lola was relieved to see.

"Sleep well?" asked Sara, plopping down on the bed near Lola.

"Like the dead. You? Aren't you starving?" asked Lola.

"I can easily skip breakfast and often do when I'm at home and can sleep in," she replied.

"Got it, no waking you up tomorrow then!" joked Lola. "Tell me, what kind of BBQ can I expect?" she asked.

"There will be many tables to eat at but we can sit anywhere, with anyone. We can even sit in the grass or wherever. So long as we pick up after ourselves. The food will be set up buffet-style under a pergola."

Lola nodded, but thought of something to ask about.

"This is totally off-topic. But when I got my admissions letter, it appeared in a plain stationery envelope. It wasn't folded like you showed me. Why is that?" asked Lola.

"The folding spell is how Travelers send letters. Witches and Wizards have owls. It seems High Elves have their own postal magic," replied Sara.

"Lady Samsara can Travel the way we do. Can all the teachers Travel?" she asked.

"Are you sure? Did she Travel on her own or did she accompany you? Who opened the door?" asked Sara.

"She mostly accompanied us. The only door I saw her open was the front door in the Main Hall. But surely she must be able to? She's the Traveling teacher!" said Lola.

"Watch her closely and you'll get your answer," mused Sara.

"Won't you tell me?" pleaded Lola.

"I'm not entirely sure myself. I've just been too lazy to think about it too much. You, on the other hand, are curious and determined. You'll get to the bottom of this!" said Sara with a wink.

Then she checked the time and said they should be getting down to the BBQ.

When they got to the pergola, most of the students and Faculty had arrived. They went hunting for their friends. The boys were showing Devlin how to propel an object with magical force. They were using popcorn and trying to get it in each other's mouths. Lenora and Clara were talking with Professor Elderberry, presumably getting to know her and inquiring about flying with her.

They grabbed a table and sat together. Which was ironic because they always sat together. The difference being the rest of their class was not also sitting with them. They took turns heading to the buffet.

When Lola went with Sara, she was pleased to see typical BBQ fare: hamburgers, regular hot dogs, Bavarian hot dogs with sauerkraut, coleslaw, potato salad, and an assortment of condiments and crudités. For dessert, which Lola would have to come back for, there were three sorts of pies: apple, pecan, and cherry.

There were water and iced tea pitchers on their table. *This is a special treat*, thought Lola, as their meals were usually only served with water, tea, and coffee. Except for breakfast, where there was freshly squeezed juice.

Most of the students were wearing gym clothes. The boys were saying they were going to play football, soccer that is, after lunch. The girls were going to tan. And Lola was looking forward to another nap.

When she went back for dessert, Tom was waiting for her.

"Did you enjoy your morning?" he asked cutting into a piece of pecan pie and asking a server to top it with ice cream.

"I fell asleep. I was really tired," said Lola trying to figure out how to fit all three pieces of pie on the same plate. Tom guessed what her dilemma was and went to get her a dinner plate instead of the tiny dessert plate.

"My hero!" she said in mock admiration. She took reasonably sized pieces and topped the apple and the pecan pie with ice cream while the cherry got whipped cream. Tom chuckled. "You eat like a starving teenage boy!"

She looked at him frostily and turned to go back to her table. He caught her arm and said, "No, wait. I'm only teasing. Don't go. It's just you're so slender. I'm wondering where you put it all."

"I've heard it all before. Don't worry. They call me Foodie now," she replied with a smirk. "When I arrived in Williamsburg, Phyllis and Jackson kept going on about how thin and pale I was. I endeavored to eat more and get some sun. I admit I never had much of an appetite until I was presented with this kind of food. Food was pretty basic with my mom," she explained.

"Okay, our ice cream is melting. There is an outdoor movie tonight. It's meant to be a surprise. Will you sit with me?" he asked.

"I would be delighted," she said with a smile.

"See you later, then," he said as he walked back to his table.

Lola went back to her own and told her friends about the outdoor movie. They already knew. Why was she even surprised?

"Do you know what it is?" she asked.

"No, that's the surprise. They have movie night every Saturday," answered Lenora.

"Well, it wasn't on the schedule," retorted Lola, her mouth full of cherry pie.

"It's a surprise for new students. The kiddies, and you two!" said James pointing at Lola and Devlin with a chuckle.

Devlin was very excited at the idea of an outdoor movie.

"We went to Movies in the Park in the summer—Mother and I. They always presented black and white classics. That's what got us into dancing!" he said nostalgically.

"Do you miss your mom?" Lola asked quietly.

"Yes, we were close. She was a stern woman, but I was her little *älskling*, which means darling," he explained. "Do you miss your mom?" he asked Lola.

"More than I thought I would. We weren't very close. My mom was very dry and reserved, always in her own head. But we were a team. Just the two of us," she said.

Devlin nodded and sighed. Then he got up to get some dessert. Lola poured herself a cup of coffee from the carafe on the table.

When everyone was finished, the boys headed to the East lawn for sports while the girls headed for the lounge chairs on the South lawn. Lola said she was going back to the room for her book. Sara asked if she could grab hers from her desk.

"Save me a chair!" she said as she ran back to the school.

She went up quickly, grabbed Sara's book, then hers and shuffled back through the door only to hit a wall. A silver-robed, very tall wall.

"Headmaster!" she yelped.

"Lola, I saw you coming up here and wondered if we might have another chat?" he suggested.

"Um, sure. But Sara is waiting for her book, and my friends are bound to wonder what happened to me. Do you mind if I go see them and come back?" said Lola.

"Yes, of course. Come directly to my office," he said and they walked down to the hall together.

"Is everything alright?" Lola asked nervously as she opened the door.

"Yes, everything is fine, don't worry. It's just a chat," he said reassuringly.

CHAPTER 30
BLOOD

LOLA SAT in the Headmaster's armchair nervously. He was pouring them some tea which meant this could go in so many directions. She knew her path was unusual but she sincerely thought her father and aunt hadn't done anything wrong. If they had, they were unaware of it.

After reading the Traveling Handbook, she was pretty sure she hadn't done anything she wasn't supposed to when she had traveled to Florence, Italy in her search for Phyllis.

"Relax, Lola, you're not in trouble," said the Headmaster.

Her eyes flew to him as he set the tea tray on the table between them.

"Did you peek into my thoughts?" she asked, worried.

"I didn't need to. The look on your face is telling enough on its own. Remember, I'm a school Headmaster, troublesome students are in my job description," he said in an attempt at humor.

Lola smiled and accepted the cup he had poured for her. Hers was a regular-sized cup, but his was larger. She blew on the tea and took a sip. It was spicy and bold, and she liked it.

"It's my favorite blend, Double Spice Masala Chai Tea," he said upon seeing her reaction.

She kept drinking her tea and waited for him to begin.

"As you know, Lola, I met with your aunt last Thursday. A delightful woman," he began and Lola smiled.

"She gave me an overview of the use of the keys in her family as far back as she could remember. Her parents never told her about attending a special school themselves and she was never expected to do so either, nor was your father. I've had someone look into our attendance archives and, indeed, no Evers have ever attended. Which begs the question as to how your family came across the keys. I've asked your aunt for a copy of your genealogical tree as we might find the answer there. That may also provide answers as to why you had a copy of the Archives. Before I forget, rest assured the book was not stolen, it simply went back to your attorney's vault."

Lola sighed with relief and nodded for him to continue.

"I've also had a conversation with the senior Mr. Radcliff. He reports that for as long as there have been Evers with keys, there have been Radcliffs as their attorneys. I've requested ancestry information about their family as well. Specifically, when they arrived in the Colonies, the United States as they are known today."

The Headmaster got up and started moving around the room as he talked. Lola drank her tea and followed his procession.

"Perhaps the Evers and the Radcliffs came over from a European country," suggested Lola.

"Yes, that's what I think. The senior Mr. Radcliff had a slight British accent. I also think the first Evers to arrive in the USA may have married a female key holder, last of her line, who somehow held on to several keys. Otherwise, one of your ancestors may have learned how to duplicate the keys at some point. That is very worrisome as any number of keys may be floating around," he said, almost to himself.

"Sir, why is it worrisome if a regular person cannot use a key to open a Traveling door?" Lola asked.

"That's true, they couldn't. From our research, we've surmised that Traveling is a gene that predisposes the carrier to utilize the magic in the keys," he explained.

"Then why is it a big deal if there are extra keys?" she asked.

"Well, because the keys are magic. They could be used for other purposes by magical beings who wish to increase their output, and that never leads to positive outcomes. If the keys were duplicated, it would have taken a very powerful sorcerer to infuse the required magic into each key. And as far as we can tell, none of the sorcerers alive today would even know where to begin to accomplish such a feat."

Lola made an *O* with her mouth and dismissed the thought that she could use the duplication spell on any magical artifact.

There was a knock at the door. The Headmaster put his cup on the table, went to answer it and ushered Devlin inside the room. He looked surprised to see Lola, as did Lola to see him.

"Perfect timing, Mr. Johansson. Please take my seat, I'll remain standing," said the Headmaster, motioning to the armchair.

"Now, the reason I called you both here is that I have some rather delicate news to share with you. Would you like some tea, Devlin?" he asked.

Devlin shook his head. The Headmaster seemed to be mulling over his news, perhaps deciding on how best to break it to them. Lola was getting anxious. He had hinted that the fact that their mothers had died within a week of one another may not have been an accident. The fact that Lola's mother had died of cancer made it a little hard to believe. But since he had not yet addressed the topic with her, that could be what he was attempting to do now.

"Devlin, your surname is that of your mother, correct?" he asked.

"Yes, sir. Since my father died before I was born and my parents were unmarried, my mother gave me her surname," explained Devlin.

"Right, I thought as much. Well, children, here it is. I have a strong feeling that you are both Simon Evers' children. Indeed, that would make you half-siblings," he stated and looked for their reaction.

"What? That's impossible!" cried Lola.

"My father died before I was born. Lola's father died when she was two years old," protested Devlin.

"He would have told me if I had a half-brother. It would have come out at the reading of his will, at the very least," said Lola, trying to stay calm and practical.

Devlin went to say something, but the Headmaster lifted a hand to silence them both.

"If you are willing, Mrs. Chevniak, our nurse, could draw blood from both of you to verify my assumption. In the meantime, here are the facts I have gathered. Our investigator has looked into a few matters including the whereabouts of your parents at the time of your births. Devlin, on the intake form at the hospital, under *Father*, your mother wrote *unknown*. We can't rule it out. You were born full-term, putting your conception sometime in September 2002. According to our research, Simon Evers was enrolled in a three-week class at The Royal Institute of Art in Stockholm around that time. He may have met and romanced the young Ms. Johansson. Remember, this was two years before he met Lola's mother. It is highly possible that Simon was never made aware of the pregnancy because Devlin's mother had no way of reaching him due to their short association. Furthermore, you are both special Travelers, which in itself is rare and usually stems from the same ancestry line. At the very least, that alone would make you distant cousins," concluded the Headmaster.

Lola and Devlin processed the news quietly at first. Then, they looked at each other and voiced their respective denials.

"But we don't look anything alike," cried Lola.

"And most of those facts add up to nothing but possibilities," said Devlin.

"Devlin, that would mean that not only are you the heir, you are also the Custodian!" said Lola, blanching a bit.

"Oh, I, no," he stammered, reaching for a response. Then, recovering, he said, "Surely the heir has to be a legitimate child?"

Lola was nodding. It really didn't matter, she thought. There was more than enough money to go around. Then warming to the idea, she added, "But if this is true, I'm sure the attorneys will figure it all out. Most importantly, you could come home and live with Phyllis and I. There's plenty of room."

"Let's not get ahead of ourselves. First the blood test, then the results," said the Headmaster.

"When can we do the test and when would we get the results?" asked Devlin anxiously.

"We can do them immediately and we'll have the results instantly," replied the Headmaster.

"How is that possible? It would take weeks to get the results back from a lab," said Lola.

"You forget this is a magic school!" he replied as he went to his desk and picked up an ancient-looking telephone with no numbers on it to dial. "Yes, won't you please send us Mrs. Chevniak? Tell her to bring her kit," he said into the receiver.

"It won't be but a moment," he said and walked back to stand near the fireplace.

"If it turns out that he is my brother, and the Custodian, can I still attend school here in the fall?" asked Lola, clearly upset about this possible development.

"Yes, you've already received your admissions letter. We wouldn't revoke it now because of this. More than ever, we would want to keep you together," said the Headmaster.

There was a brisk knock and the door opened. Mrs. Chevniak made a slight curtsy to the Headmaster and headed towards Lola and Devlin. Her *kit* was not at all what Lola had expected. There were no needles or tubes. She took out two sterilized pouches which each contained a small surgical tool to prick their fingers. She squeezed out a few drops of Lola's blood on the glass plate that was in the pouch. She did the same to Devlin. Then she took a drop of blood from each and combined them on another glass plate. She waved her hand over their combined blood and it turned green.

"You are related, close enough that you should not be married and have children," she said, but she wasn't finished.

Then she took out two more sterilized pouches. These had what looked like writing quills. She dipped the first quill in Lola's blood. She took out a piece of parchment, closed her eyes, and began writing. When she opened her eyes, she showed the parchment to Lola. "Are these the names of your parents?" she asked. Lola swallowed and read,

"*Elaine Sophie Harris and Simon Bartholomew Evers.*" There was a frog lodged in Lola's throat and all she could do was nod.

Mrs. Chevniak took the other quill and another parchment and repeated the process with Devlin's blood. "Are these the names of your parents?" she asked.

Devlin took the paper and stared at it. Lola strained in his direction to see what was written.

He read it out loud for all to hear, "*Alice Maja Johansson and Simon Bartholomew Evers.*"

The End

If you enjoyed this book, please consider leaving a review on <u>Amazon</u>, <u>Goodreads</u>, or <u>Bookbub</u>.

Reviews help me reach new readers and improve my craft.

Read The Time Walker, the next book in *The Evers Series*!

Join my Newsletter for writing updates, sales and giveaways!

ABOUT THE AUTHOR

Positive, uplifting books and stories.

Marie-Hélène Lebeault is the author of *The Evers Series, Clarity Castle, What Happens Next? Readers Decide Which Story Becomes a Book, the Blood Magick Trilogy, Holiday Shifters, Ghost Stories, Defenders of the Realm, Utopia, Chronicles of the Starborne Cadets*, as well as a series of picture books called Fairy Grandmother. She lives in Canada with her grown children.

www.mhlebeault.com

Follow on Social Media, she'd love to hear from you!

facebook.com/mhlebeaultauthor

x.com/mhlebeault

instagram.com/mhlebeault

amazon.com/author/mhlebeault

bookbub.com/authors/marie-helene-lebeault

goodreads.com/mhlebeault

linkedin.com/in/mhlebeault

tiktok.com/@mhlebeaultauthor

ALSO BY THE AUTHOR

Legends Reborn (Fairytale Retellings)

A Curse of Snow and Ash

A Curse of Thorns and Slumber

A Curse of Glass and Shadows

A Curse of Iron and Roses

A Curse of Briars and Hearts

The Chronicles of the Starborne Cadets

Stars Beyond Realms

Shadows of Orion

Echoes of the Void

The Nebula's Heart

The Starborne Paradox

Defenders of the Realm

A Journey to Power

The Quest for the Emerald Rattleback

A Summer of Discovery

The Quest for the Sacred Tree

A Summer of Opposites

The Quest for the Phantom Feather

A Summer of Courage

The Quest for the Kraken's Ink

A Summer of Destiny

The Quest for the Cursed Mirrors

A Summer of Unity

Defenders of the Realm - Special Edition Hardcover Set

The Evers Series

The Ancestors' Key

The Academy

The Time Walker

The World Jumper

5th Anniversary Edition Omnibus

The Traveler's Handbook

The Lost Key

Blood Magick Trilogy

The Blood Mage

Blood Magick

Blood Legacy

Extended Edition Omnibus

Standalones

Clarity Castle

What Happens Next?

Ghost Stories

Holiday Shifters

Echoes of Tomorrow

Utopia

Picture Books

Fairy Grandmother: Millie Goes to Antarctica

Fairy Grandmother: Millie Goes to the North Pole

Fairy Grandmother: Millie Goes to China

Fairy Grandmother: Millie Goes to Africa

(Also available in French, Spanish, German, and Italian)